Call of the Mandrake

F.R. Jameson

Copyright © 2019 F.R. Jameson

All rights reserved.

ISBN: 9781655607790

To V and E, with love, always.

All Ghostly Shadows tales can be read as stand-alone, but they all take place in the same universe.
Sort of…

Also by F.R. Jameson in paperback

Ghostly Shadows
Death at the Seaside
Certain Danger
Won't You Come Save Me

Screen Siren Noir
Diana Christmas
Eden St. Michel
Alice Rackham

Short Stories
Confined Spaces

1. THE VILLAGE WHICH SHUT ITSELF OFF

I like to think that there were other reasons for me accompanying Ludo Carstairs to the village of Beddnic, rather than simply my ability to pilot the dinghy. Given how momentous and life changing that trip was for me, I tell myself that there were greater forces at play. That it wasn't only my skill at wielding a tiller. Obviously, there's fate and destiny and marvellous cosmic forces, but I also try to convince myself that there were more human reasons why I was present as well. That I was a crucial part of the mission, and not merely the taxi driver.

By that point, Ludo was already The Golden Boy of The Organisation. In an incident like this, right at home on the British Isles, then he was always going to be sent in. But I choose to believe I have my uses. That I provided a useful sounding board to him, that I calmed him down from his most excitable ideas, that I built a bridge between him and the less brilliant people he met. (Which basically constituted everybody else on the planet.) Obviously I'd gone through the training he had and had a certain expertise in these matters myself, and so I wasn't only there to pilot the bloody boat.

Beddnic sits on the south west coast of Wales. A fishing village; a strange – surely deliberately – remote conurbation. Battered by the winds and rain of the Irish Sea every day, it was a collection of forty-one pretty much identical terraced houses. Servicing them was a tiny village shop, which existed in the converted front room of one of those houses; and a local pub, which was the sole commercially built premises in Beddnic and stood much bigger and wider than any other building. Even a mile out to sea, it loomed as if it was bullying all around it. Although, as we got closer, you could see that its white paintjob had enjoyed better days, and that the doors and windows would long ago have needed replacing in a town where everybody *didn't* know everyone else.

There was a one track road which looped around from the A4507, before looping out again to the exact point it started. No one had ever accidently found themselves in Beddnic. It was a place where people either chose to go, or bypassed without realising it was there.

At first glance, it was hard to imagine anybody living in such an isolated place. Yet somehow a whole community had burst through a crack in the rocks and taken root in this small stormy cove. It was the type of geographic location where sunlight only really appeared through a distant haze and every colour was a different variation of grey. The kind of town which minded its own business and expected the rest of the world to return the favour. And as if to prove that point, for the last three weeks, it had closed itself off completely from any outside prying eyes.

That one track road was blocked off by two immobilised lorries. It was at a point where the road dipped off a cliff face one side, and into a rut of a small rocky valley the other, making it impossible for any vehicle to go around. Those who had tried to walk it were met a good mile away from town by the women of Beddnic. It was as if they had been placed there as sentries, or guards. These women were firm: they told whoever attempted access that it was in their best interests to turn around. The message was relayed so firmly, it almost counted as a threat. Obviously all this caught its own type of attention, and three days ago a helicopter diverted to fly over had a flare fired at it. Whatever was happening in Beddnic, they obviously didn't want snooping outside eyes observing.

"What's all this got to do with us?" asked Ludo Carstairs.

The two of us stood side by side only a few miles up the coast from the village; the collars of our coats raised against the drizzle. Neither of us had had the foresight to bring an umbrella, which given this was Wales, seemed particularly foolish.

Ludo's watery blue eyes peered upwards and yet undeniably commanding at The Chief. "To me this has the ring of cult behaviour at its most stereotypical. Remote location and insular inhabitants gradually shutting themselves off from the outside world. I'm sure it's highly worrying for their loved ones, but how does it fall into our remit, precisely? They're probably preparing for the apocalypse, which they no doubt imagine will come a week Tuesday, not long after lunch. Once the sun rises the next day, they'll want to know the football scores again – mark my words."

The Chief had learned to be patient with Ludo's condescension. He was a big man who may have been the most solid looking human being I'd ever met. When he spoke, his voice was a low rumble – like he really was a block of sentient rock.

"It's more than that," he told us. "You both need to read the paperwork. Before they sealed themselves off, there were rumours circulating locally that there was something very wrong in Beddnic. Stories of men disappearing. Not just the ones we have the police reports for, but numerous others afterwards. And then, well – it's as if the town decided that the outside world couldn't offer any help, and so stopped asking."

Ludo shook his head. "Men, or indeed women, disappearing could of course be individuals snapping to their senses: those who've decided that this particular cult isn't for them. Too many robes, or too few sandals, or they wanted to get away before the wicker man was actually lit. I ask you again, why oh why have you dragged me here? Why have you dragged *us* here?"

I glanced down at Ludo (I was a head height taller than him myself). Part of me wondered whether to be annoyed that he'd only included me as an afterthought, or happy that he'd thought to include me at all.

There was surely a time when The Chief, a former army man, would have exploded with invective at any insubordination. Let alone the constant challenges which came from Ludo. With a hardened, impenetrable stare from his blue eyes, he peered at Ludo and waited for him to finish.

"What makes it interesting to us, Carstairs, is that we also have the coincidence of The Mandrake."

Ludo's eyebrow raised, but it was me who asked the

question. "I'm sorry, sir. What's The Mandrake?"

"The HMS Mandrake was a high-tech communications vessel which sank mysteriously in the Second World War. It hadn't long been launched on its maiden voyage, but disappeared from the radar a few miles from where we're standing now. The nearest town to this disaster was, of course, Beddnic."

"I do love it when people talk in riddles." Ludo gave me a crooked grin. "It's what I do and I know that others find it immensely irritating, but myself – I love it. In a jiffy, our beloved leader here is going join these dots together, Garris, and then we'll find out what we're really dealing with."

The Chief grinned at the praise, his teeth big and slab-like. "Four months ago, the sunken Mandrake started to transmit to the outside world. It is emitting two messages, one that's strong and is an SOS, and another fainter and more localised – which we cannot determine the purpose of. The ship is a couple of miles underwater and, all these years later, it took us a while to recognise what on earth we were hearing. But it's The Mandrake alright. It's transmitting something or other at low-range, a signal that would only be able to sustain itself for a couple of miles. So basically, it's serving as an incredibly local radio station. It's sending out this signal and suddenly, the citizens of this village of Beddnic – its sole audience – are behaving strangely. So strangely that The Organisation has been called in."

An ice cold gust of wind blew through us, sending shiver-inducing rain into our faces. Neither of us lost The Chief's gaze.

"Specifically, what kind of ship did you say The Mandrake was?" asked Ludo.

"A high-tech and highly experimental

communications vessel."

Ludo practically gave an eye-roll. "There's a vague British Intelligence-type description for you. What then is a 'highly experimental communications vessel'?"

"As I understand it, The Mandrake was the one of its kind. It sank and there wasn't time before the end of the war to build another. Records are understandably patchy. We don't tend to immortalise our failures."

We were stood the other side of the bay from Beddnic, a good seven miles away. But Ludo stared to the sea as if he could peer around the rocks and into Beddnic itself.

"What do you think, Garris?" he asked me.

"We're here and it most definitely sounds intriguing."

"Intriguing – that is indeed the perfect word for it." He grinned at The Chief. "I take it all back. I'm glad you brought us here, after all. *We're* glad you brought us here."

After the flare incident, there wasn't much appetite for heading in by helicopter. Besides, as Ludo pointed out, that would show immediately we were connected to the military, when really we needed to go in there as friends. The friendliest seeming transport we could get at such short notice was a small rubber dingy with an outboard motor. If I'm honest, the coastguard didn't look overly confident as he presented it, but he assured us that the sea was calm enough that December day that the odds were in our favour of probably making it.

Of course, Ludo himself didn't know how to pilot any vessel – it would have been an altogether too practical skill for him – and so I did it. Two agents of the uncanny going into a remote and possibly dangerous location, when our organisation's guidelines (which, admittedly, were ignored far more often than they were obeyed), stipulated that in such circumstance it should only be one. The two of us skirted across the grey, murky, incredibly cold depths of the Irish Sea, already certain that whatever greeting we got in Beddnic, it wasn't really going to be a warm one.

2. THE WOMAN ON THE BEACH

"Get away! Get away!"

We were still a hundred yards from the pebbled beach, but the young woman's voice was a passionate, desperate shriek over the waves.

I squinted as best I could; the wind was squally and blew ice cold water into my face from every conceivable direction. The woman was dressed in jeans and a thick black duffel coat. Her long, raven black hair fell loose and was wind-swept over her shoulders, with her fringe flicking up and blown side to side in the gusts. Incredibly, despite otherwise being wrapped warm, she was barefoot on the shingle.

"Go away!" she screamed again. "Get away! You have to turn around!"

Clearly she wasn't old, but her voice as it carried on the wind sounded beaten and hoarse, as if she'd been screaming at the sea for a dozen years.

The outboard motor whirred and the waves bounced us around with an almost malicious intensity. Ludo's expression was stoic, but he couldn't hide the green tint to his cheeks. We were only fifty yards away, far too late to turn around. Still she tried to convince us – her anguished, desperate voice echoing.

"Get away!"

As we got closer and I knew that the danger of capsizing had passed, I studied her. I could see the tears creating a thin sheen on her face, adding lines that shouldn't yet have found their way onto her youthful skin. She was bending double at the waist, seemingly furious and overwrought that we weren't listening to her.

"Don't you understand? You have to get away! Please! You have to keep away!"

She didn't quite drop to her knees as I kept my hand steady and steered the dinghy onto land, but it was like a great weight slumped onto her from above. As if she was being pressed upon by an awful external force and was almost ready to buckle onto the pebbles.

Ludo had sat portside and so of course was first off the dinghy. He scrambled a little uncertainly at first up the soaked shingle, reaching his hands out to prevent a fall – before finding his balance and striding confidently up the beach: very much the proud Englishman. Willpower is what he later attributed it to, but I don't truly understand how he managed to ignore what must have been a fully churning stomach while he played the part of a visiting ambassador, rather than a bloke who needed to find a quiet place to puke.

As for me, I never manage to locate such grace at those moments. (Or indeed, any moments.) Instead, as I tried to steady myself and step onto the beach, I slipped and dropped knees first into the incoming tide. The waves of the December Irish Sea lapped remorselessly over my arse and waist. I don't think I had ever felt such intense coldness.

Not that Ludo noticed my predicament. He was up the beach and grinning, as if he'd done nothing more strenuous than take a post-lunch promenade. The woman – and if I had to guess then, I'd have said she was early twenties at most – stared at him as if her eyes were playing fancies with her.

"Good afternoon, madam." Ludo offered that uneven, yet charming, smile of his. "My name is Ludo Carstairs and this is my companion, Michael Garris. You may, or may not, believe this, but we've actually come here today to check that things are going well in Beddnic. That all is as it should be. We've come in peace, as it were. We've come because we care. You might consider yourselves done with the outside world, but I'm here to tell you that the outside world isn't done with you."

She stared at him as if nothing he said made any sense; she clearly couldn't follow him at all. For a second, I feared that she was a Welsh speaker – that she knew enough English to yell at us to leave, but not much more – and we were going to be two stereotypical Englishmen trying to make ourselves understood by speaking in annoyingly louder and louder voices.

By now I'd managed to extricate myself from the water, marching up behind Ludo, soaked and shivering.

"I'm Beryl," the woman's voice was little more than a murmured croak. "And I'm sorry, but you really do have to go."

Under the grey foreboding sky, and with tears on her cheeks and emotion cut through her face, she undoubtedly didn't look her best. Yet within seconds I knew that Beryl was one of the most beautiful women I had ever seen. Naturally black hair, alabaster flawless skin and eyes which shone both wide and passionate. She was a tall lady and athletically built. Next to Ludo, she was an Amazonian.

"Beryl, please," he sounded as sincere and ingratiating as he ever got. Normally he tried to bulldoze his way through objections and obstacles. "I promise you we are here to help. Or at least to talk. If you've all decided on a whim you've had enough of the outside world, then so be it. If that's your choice, we will respect that. But I have a suspicion that there's more going on here than a desire for communal solitude. If I'm right, then please talk to us. Trust me, we are two men who can help, no matter what is happening. No matter how strange it might be."

The three of us were no longer alone. I don't know if Ludo had noticed it on our arrival, so fixed was he on Beryl, but she wasn't the only person paying attention to us. On the three little streets which made up the village, doors had opened. They'd been pulled back silently, almost synchronised, and now coming towards the beach was a party of women. It seemed there was at least one from every house in Beddnic. No men at all, just forty or so women – young and old, tall and short, thin and rounded – making their way down the sloping thin tarmacked strip to join us on the shingle.

Not one appeared remotely pleased to see us.

All of them had faces which showed the strain of worry; they carried bags under their eyes which suggested many nights' lost sleep.

The lady at the front, whom all the others seemed to naturally fall behind, was in her fifties and big boned.

A tough maternal seeming figure, wrapped in a grey cardigan that she wore like armour. She carried an expression of determination I hadn't seen matched in even the most experienced agent, and possessed a natural steel which would undoubtedly make grown men quail. Her skin was pale and weather-beaten, and her hair was wind-swept and untamed as if it hadn't seen a brush in days. Otherwise, she would have been the perfect headmistress for a particularly strict prep school.

She was marching towards us, leading the pack, a snarl apparent from thirty feet away. This village seemingly only had the single facial expression to go around.

"You stupid English bastards don't listen to warnings then?" she yelled.

"No, madam." Ludo took a step away from Beryl and sauntered towards this new lady and her party – recognising true authority when he encountered it. "Not listening to warnings is something I take a great deal of pride in. Please, let me make the introductions. My name is Ludo Carstairs and this is my colleague, Michael Garris."

Her cardigan stretched right the way to her feet. It was baggy and seemed comfortable and lived in. It was also far more spacious than it first appeared. She pulled her right hand from inside it and drew out a large hunting rifle.

I did my best not to stare straight at the weapon, to try and meet the woman's gaze instead. To get through to her that we were all people here and the consequences of violence would be dreadful on so many levels. But if I had to guess, I'd say it was a .375 H&H. It was old however, and decidedly worn. In the coastal air of Beddnic, it would be a nightmare to keep in working order. We could only hope that over the years, she hadn't. Although, she didn't strike me as the kind of woman who would skimp on the hard tasks.

Slowly she raised the barrel, pointing it directly at Ludo's face. "Fine then," she barked. "If you won't listen to us, will you listen to this?"

Both Ludo and I slowly raised our hands. Somehow he manged to hold onto his smile, although it was a bit more abashed now.

3. LUDO IN THE FACE OF THE SHOTGUN

"I think," the lady told us, her jaw set firm, "if we're not going to have any problems today, you need to get into that toy bloody boat of yours, head onto the water and return to wherever the hell you came from. How does that sound?"

Beryl's tones – despite the obvious strain of emotion – had been softer, mellifluous. The kind of accent so pleasing to the ears that advertising companies would lean on it to sell their wares. In contrast, this lady's voice was much harsher; it was as if her larynx was coated with salt water and cockles.

My hands stretched skywards, which given I was already the tallest person on the beach made me feel like a South Seas Island's statue. I stared around for a sympathetic face. There was maybe a flicker of the eyelashes from Beryl – a brief flash of empathy – before she settled into the same contemptuous, wary fury as the others.

"Why?" asked Ludo. He sounded provocatively

chipper.

The gun-wielding lady said, "I'm sorry?"

I gave a silent inward sigh of relief at the business end of the rifle being focused so exclusively on him. Even if he was much more likely to talk himself into being shot.

"Why do you want us gone?"

"You don't need to know the why, little man. No, you need to get away from here and do it this instant. Before I lose my patience."

He nodded once and then lowered his hands, pushing them through his unruly dirty blonde hair as he did. In an instant he transformed his demeanour from a man being held at gunpoint, to an ebullient guest at a dinner party – one who's maybe had a cocktail too many. Whistling a solitary cheery note, he rocked relaxed onto his heels and gave her his fullest, most crookedly charming smile.

"No," he said softly, "I don't think so. Lovely as the offer is, I didn't enjoy my ride in here enough that I'd immediately want to take the return trip."

"What?" The gun jumped in her hands, seeming – of its own accord – to get an inch or so closer to his forehead.

"Madam, please, I'm trying to do this as painlessly and politely as possible, but I said 'No'. I'm looking at you, eyeball to eyeball, and I don't think you want to shoot me and I don't think you mean to shoot me. You want me gone, certainly. That is abundantly clear. And I can see that from your point of view the old, trusted rifle seems the best way to achieve that aim. But, if I'm frank, I really don't believe you'll use it."

Her face remained hard and creased with fury. To me she appeared more than capable of pulling the trigger.

"You could be wrong," she snarled at him. "And if you are, it would be the last mistake you ever made."

"And yet, you haven't shot me." Ludo beamed. "Come now, I know that as far as you're concerned, we're two English simpletons who've washed in on a ridiculous little boat. You have no idea whether anyone knows where we are, or even how much they would care. If you were so minded, you could easily blow us both away and leave us on the beach for the tide and gulls to dispose of. Yet we both know you're not going to do that, don't we?" He took a step forward so that his forehead almost rested on the endless black of the barrel. "So, please, put away this impressive firearm and let us talk. That's all we ask. Take the time to tell us what is going on here and we will do our utmost to help you."

The lady glared at us, the rifle clasped firmly. Her gaze was more pitying towards me, as if already considering what it would involve to put up with Ludo for the long term. However, it was only a few seconds before – with a tired sigh – she lowered the weapon to point at the beach.

"You smart, runty, little bastard," she whispered.

"Pleased to meet you! As I said, my name is Ludo Carstairs and this strapping – slightly dripping – chap to my right is my colleague, Michael Garris. And you are?"

She stared away in disgust. "If you're going to call me anything, you can call me Myfanwy."

"Myfanwy, it is."

All the women had looked hurt and disheartened at the bluff of the rifle failing, but few more than Beryl. "Sunset is in half an hour!" She spoke with fearful urgency.

"I know, I know." Myfanwy shook her head wearily and then gave a glance over her shoulder at the other women. Perhaps she was hunting for a helpful suggestion, but there was a reason she'd become their de facto leader. "Does anyone else want a go at making these idiots listen to sense?"

"What happens at sunset?" Ludo asked. "Vampires? Werewolves? A variety of ghostly visitations? Believe me, we are both incredibly open minded."

"You wouldn't understand."

"Garris!" Ludo called. "Why don't you give the good lady Myfanwy a brief overview of our curriculum vitae?"

Moronically I still had my hands raised. I lowered them with a bashful grin, hoping everybody was too preoccupied to notice me making a fool of myself.

I cleared my throat. "We work for a privately funded, not for profit, organisation which investigates the uncanny. We're well known in the right circles and are frequently subcontracted to governments – which is the case right now. Myself and my colleague, Ludo, are both investigators. Grade one level. As such we are hugely experienced with the odd, the inexplicable and the unusual. And where we can, we help."

Myfanwy, despite having threatened to shoot us, had the amused and dismissive smirk of someone who can't quite believe what they're hearing. It was a look I was all too familiar with. "So you're like those bozos off *The X Files* then?"

"Yes," nodded Ludo. "Except that we have less good haircuts."

"And you're here to help us?" The eagerness in Beryl's voice was impossible to hide.

Her enthusiasm was shut down immediately by a sudden growl from Myfanwy. The smirk had been fleeting and her features now settled back into a hard wariness. Behind her the other women wore the same expression. I'd had the chance to count them all and there were thirty-nine women in total, ranging from old ladies to teenagers – each with the same tired, hurt face.

"What makes you think we have anything 'uncanny' here?" Myfanwy demanded. "What on Earth makes you presume that we would want your help? Or that two *men* could help us?"

The business end of the rifle was resting on the pebbles, and she leant her full weight into it. Staring at us with her harsh grey, headmistress eyes.

With a flourish, Ludo waved his right hand through the air, as if preparing the reveal of a magic trick at The Palladium. All it took was two steps and he seemed to wave direct at each woman in turn, like they were all sitting in the royal circle.

Ludo riposted, "What makes you think you can hide whatever is going on here and the outside world won't care? I know that answering a question with another question is the most frightful bad manners, but I'm going to say that we're beyond such niceties now. You've blocked off the road in here, fired a flare at a passing helicopter and anyone who arrives by sea you threaten with a rifle. I don't think I'm reaching when I presume that there's something very strange going on here. Nor is it arrogance on my part when I say that we could probably help you with it."

"You say two *men* can't help you," I added, "but that makes me wonder, where are the men of this town?"

"Quite right, Garris." Ludo took a final step towards her. Making an audience of one. "Where are they, Myfanwy?"

A silence fell, one that echoed uncomfortably against the crashing of the waves. It struck me that there were no gulls either. We hadn't heard any since we entered the cove. It was as if the sounds of the beach were missing a crucial component: an orchestra with no violins.

The women shared little glances from the corners of their eyes, a full blown discussion taking place that we weren't party to. I hoped they were deciding how much they were willing to tell us, rather than simply the best way to dispose of us.

Myfanwy in no way entered this debate. Her eyes were locked on Ludo, her jaw set, her entire expression unyielding.

Even Beryl's pleading stare, first in my direction and then at the older lady, made not a jot of difference. Myfanwy barely gave any indication she'd even seen it.

An icy wind blew into the cove, my damp legs shivered and only bloody minded concentration stopping my teeth from chattering.

It was Beryl who broke the impasse, Beryl who shattered that uneasy silence. Passion rising to the surface, she yelled: "What are we going to do? They have to be gone by sunset! They have to!"

Ludo's gaze shot to her. "What happens at sunset, Beryl? Please tell me."

She ignored him, just staring at the leader of this community. "We have to make them go! We have to!"

For a second it seemed as if Myfanwy was considering raising the rifle again and seeing if renewed threats would work. Instead, she slowly shook her head.

"I can't help it if they won't listen to sense, girl! How

can I help it if they're as stubborn and as stupid as any man?"

"But, please!" Beryl wept, and this time she did drop to her knees on the jagged shingle of the beach. As if all the world's problems had crashed down on her shoulders at once.

Myfanwy kept her attention fixed on Ludo. Recognising that he had (as usual) put himself in charge and she had no need to debate with me.

"Come again tomorrow," she told him.

"I'm sorry?"

"First thing in the morning, can you come then? You can bring your little boat, or you can fly in on a big red helicopter for all I care. We won't stop you. Come back tomorrow and we will tell you all then. But please – if you know what's good for you – you have to go now."

"Because of the sunset?"

She glanced accusingly at the weeping, crumpled Beryl. All the women of the town seemed to be on the beach, but not one of them had moved to comfort her.

"What's the weather going to be tomorrow, Garris?" Ludo asked.

I had no idea, but knew what he wanted to hear. "The last forecast I read, it was going to be stormy. It would be hard to come in by boat. With the wind tunnel of this cove, it'd be difficult to come in by helicopter too. Probably impossible, in fact."

"Fine!" Myfanwy barked. "Come in by road, we'll clear it for you. But please, go now. It'll be safer for you than staying here. Much safer."

"We can help you today, you know?" Ludo's voice was soothing. "We really can."

"So you say, but we'd really rather talk about it

tomorrow."

Ludo nodded once and with his big, beaming, crooked smile, he turned and strolled towards the dinghy. My legs felt heavy and numb, which is why I didn't immediately go with him.

The tide was in and we'd only made it about fifteen foot from the dinghy, so it took him mere moments to get to it. Then with that grin in place – one that was equidistant between ingratiating and mischievous – and his eyes locked onto Myfanwy's, he reached into his jacket and pulled out a small, serrated blade I didn't know he had. Calmly, and without obvious effort, he gutted the rubber sides of the boat.

It deflated with the sound of a death rattle.

"Apologies for that!" He called to us in a singsong voice. "The thing is I'm so very, very intrigued to see for myself what happens at sunset!"

"You stupid, stupid man!" Myfanwy raised the rifle again. This time as if she might possibly use it. "You damn fool of a man!"

4. MANACLED

At the top of the beach, a metal post had been cemented deep into the ground, presumably so that little boats could be dragged up and tied to it. Over time it had become battered and rusty. Thousands of boats had no doubt been chained there over the last hundred years. It made sense for it to be on a beach like this.

I didn't know why a heavy-duty set of iron manacles were suddenly wrapped around it though.

Ludo whipping that knife out had brought the rifle very much back into play. Not even he was prepared to gamble that Myfanwy wouldn't use it this time.

"Whatever happens," she hissed at us, "you brought this on yourselves. I want you to remember that. I want you stupid fools to bear that in mind."

It was a girl named Carys – a slim and slight teenager with long red hair – who was sent off to get the manacles. She didn't need to be told where they were.

Ludo, hands in the air, persisted in stating his position. "I'd greatly appreciate it if, rather than anything drastic, we could talk."

"Drastic?" she scoffed. "Don't you witter to me about drastic, little man! The time for talking is over. Sunset is in no more than fifteen minutes off."

Again he asked: "What happens at sunset?"

She lowered the rifle and took a step towards him, the result wasn't any less menacing. "You'll see. You'll bloody see."

The iron manacles were obviously heavy, but Carys must have been stronger than she looked. The chain was somewhat rusted yet, compared to the metal post itself, it appeared a completely different generation. While the locking mechanism actually gleamed in that weak sunlight; shiny, clearly replaced only recently.

Myfanwy may have lowered the rifle again, but Ludo and I still had the combined force of all those women to contend with. As a pack they pushed us with their will. They had a frightened urgency to them that was impossible to resist.

At least half the women wept, Beryl in particular almost screamed with anxious tears. Her pale skin trembling with tangible fear; her forehead crinkling as she shot worried glances at the horizon. The sky was slate grey. My astronomer father would have bemoaned it as ten-tenths cloud. But, if you squinted hard enough, you could see the faint white of the sun sinking faster and faster.

Myfanwy didn't weep like the others, or appear likely to. Instead she held the determination steady in her grey eyes. Eyes the same threatening colour as the clouds.

We had to sit on the shingle and our wrists were clamped tight in the manacles either side of the post. Chained together in the cold and damp. Night was coming in and my trousers remained wet. Not that that was high on my list of problems anymore.

"In the morning, we can talk about this – is that correct?" Ludo hadn't quit with his bonhomie, a fact which clearly annoyed Myfanwy.

"If you live that long," she told him.

Even forced to sit on the ground and chained, he managed a commanding gaze upwards. "Do we at least get a hint as to what comes next? I'm guessing your worry isn't that the tide will come in far enough to drown us both?"

"The tide doesn't come in this far."

"What then? Please enlighten us. As I've already said, we're very credulous men."

"Maybe. But you're still men."

With a fearful glance over her shoulder at the approaching tide, she turned and walked away. That look was actually the most distressing aspect so far for me. What the hell was coming that such a woman would be frightened of it?

Perhaps even Ludo was lost in anticipation and anxiety. It was so rare for him to gift anyone else the last word, that there was generally a good reason.

"We've done our best for you two," Myfanwy yelled at us. "That's all we can do."

With that she, and the other women of Beddnic, marched away as one. The sun had nearly vanished and every woman there, Beryl included, hurried from us – seemingly desperate to be indoors.

Beryl's last words to us had been a tear-laden: "You should have gone. You really should have left while you had the chance."

We watched them all disappear. Two wet and cold Englishmen wondering what the hell they'd got into.

As the sun dropped below the horizon and a shadowy darkness fell, I heard Ludo utter: "Well, this is a bit of a pickle, isn't it, Garris? The full relish in fact."

They were the last clear words I can recall him speaking that night.

5. THE FIRST NIGHT

It came upon us swift and invisible.

The waves kept crashing in, yet suddenly the only sound I could hear was screaming.

It was a hundred voices – no, more than that: a million impassioned, tortured, suffering, giddy voices yelling into my ears at once. A dreadful cacophony of noise, a horrific orchestra of suffering. So many voices wrapped together in pain, yet each one of them totally distinct. It was the cry of a multitude of souls, and it seemed like I could pick out each and every voice and understand its own personal suffering. As if I could grasp each individual's personal pain; every one of them was relaying his agony just to me. I felt responsible and guilty for everything these poor men had suffered.

The panic I experienced was immediate. My eyes burned and my entire vision was suffused with red. I squinted, jammed my eyelids tight together, but all I could see was the world – that cold beach, the barren cove, the distant sea – in various shades of blood red.

It was as if my forehead had been slashed open and a trail of thick blood was pouring over my pupils. Or as if every capillary behind my retinas had burst and stained my vision scarlet forever.

Desperately I stared over at Ludo, hoping that his constant calmness would have an effect on me. That I could feed off it, steady myself from it. Nothing affected Ludo, he showed the world a sanguine face in the most bizarre of circumstances. Surely, he was going to be okay. He'd be dealing with whatever this was. Bringing his own cold personal logic to bear in a way that would carry us both through.

But no, Ludo was sprawled on the pebbles, his arms and legs thrashing about as if struck by epilepsy. His left wrist tearing and thrashing against the restraint of the manacles. I might have been mistaken in the stained world before me, but I think there was foam coming from his lips.

In an instant, it was like my mouth was burning too. I could not only see red, but feel it as well. It was as if my mouth was aflame, with something stuffed forcibly into my throat. Hot ashes, that's what my fevered mind told me it tasted of, what it smelled of. Burnt and charred flakes, crammed smouldering into my mouth.

I didn't want to think about what it might be, but of course, the most frightened part of my mind leapt to its own conclusion.

It was people, the burnt remains of human beings. Someone (*something*) had torn open the door of a crematorium oven, shovelled out a smoking pile of ashes and forced them smouldering between my lips. I could hear the screams of the people themselves as their ashes burnt into me, as they filled my mouth and choked my throat. They screamed louder, more intense, as their flaming remains suffocated me towards my own death.

Part of me wanted to swallow. My mouth was too full and I felt too weak to spit it all out. Despite my fears, my only response was to swallow, to clear my airwaves by filling my stomach with the charred remains of screaming men. But each time I tried, a gag reflex kicked in. I didn't have enough strength to spit, but involuntarily I could retch into my mouth again and again. My mouth was full and getting fuller, but there was no way I could eat the desiccated remains of human beings. No matter how loudly my rational mind yelled that it was the only way to save myself, I couldn't. So my mouth kept filling with ashes as my windpipe clogged and I couldn't scream anymore.

But then a scream did come. With a crash of the waves, my mouth cleared and a scream roared forth, carried on a gasp of wonderful salty air.

Through the crimson gauze, the sea appeared suddenly beautiful. The waves were deliciously tempting. It was warm. I could tell that from where I sat, the sea was hot and alluring. My faulty vision showed it as red, but I realised that wasn't because of my broken capillaries. The sea was red because it had heated to a beautiful temperature. Somehow the water had become tropical, was an ocean to bathe in naked.

I screamed again. Managing to be louder than the cacophony of noise in my head, the musical beating of the waves. A thump-thump-thump that resembled a comforting heartbeat. I jerked my arm to try and free myself, but instead fell onto the shingle: feeling each pebble, stone and rock sear its way into me. Scorching my skin, sinking right through my flesh, burning to my bones. It was like I was being melted; as if I was being incinerated alive both inside and out.

Next to me Ludo was screaming. I roared out as well. Both of us so loud we drowned out a million other cries of suffering.

Paradoxically, the sea now appeared cool. It was a green lagoon of sanctuary. Everything else was red and blood-stained. A hell-scape that burnt and injured me – which would kill Ludo and I – but the sea was placid, it was a place where both of us could be safe.

I knew I had to get to it. The gently lapping water was going to save me. It was a certainty that I absolutely knew to be true. I had to get to the sea. Surrender myself to it, stay there forever. The sea would look after me, it would be my home, my barricade against the burning world. I had to get to the sea.

With every ounce of strength I possessed, I lurched forward. But the searing metal of the manacle snatched me back. Crying with frustration I clutched it, yanked at it, tried to break it and – when I couldn't get any purchase – to snap my own wrist off. Somehow, despite the ashes starting to fill my mouth again, I managed to find space for my own hand. Desperately trying to chew through the skin so I could save myself.

I had to be in the sea. It was the only thing which made any sense, I had to get down the beach and into the water. Risk my feet against the searing pebbles so I could reach the tranquil coolness.

The other side of the post, Ludo was on his knees pulling at the manacles, his chest heaving with effort. As if he could rip the links apart with his untapped might, break them so we could both escape into the water and be safe.

But the metal, despite its rust, was too fucking

strong! We couldn't find any give, I couldn't gnaw off my own hand, since the ashes constrained my frantic efforts, and so we both roared with soul-tearing frustration.

I don't know when I realised there were others around us.

In my red, hell-burnt gaze, I think I was gradually aware of heavy boots approaching my side. In the discordant screams echoing through my ears, I heard them crushing the shingle.

Terror assailed me from every direction. My desire to get into the water was overwhelming, as was my fear of everything on the land.

I saw a grey man go past me. Grey when everything around him was vivid red. He was big and surly, with unkempt dark hair and unshaven jowls. Wrapped in a heavy jacket and waterproofs, he didn't walk past me, he stumbled and staggered.

In the strange burning air of that beach, I felt speckles of cool beautiful water, droplets from his jacket as he went by – a gentle rain onto my upturned face. The most incredible, refreshing shower.

My lungs roaring, I stared across the beach, desperate to be in the water, wanting it with every part of my being.

There were about three dozen men coming up the beach towards us. Grey, cool looking men, emerging from the green lagoon of the cove.

How were they able to touch the water and I wasn't? My wrist twisted around in the shackle, cutting grooves into the skin. I wanted to be Houdini and find a way to effortlessly escape.

None of the men walked with any purpose. They all lurched and stumbled on uncertain feet. Their sodden clothes made them heavy, their movement further hampered by the blankness of their eyes.

It's hard for me to recall exactly what I saw and what was filled in by my imagination later (although when I compared notes with Ludo, he had much the same recollection), but it seemed that everything I saw on land was red, apart from the men who – as they got closer – seemed more white and blotchy. They looked like they'd been submerged in the sea a long time, the waves taking all the dreadful heat from their skin.

These were the dead men of Beddnic, staggering up the beach towards the town they'd once called home.

Their gait was all the same, their skin was the same, their eyes were the same – white and empty. At least those of them who still had eyes. A good dozen of them merely had empty black sockets, their tasty eyeballs obviously having proved too tempting to passing denizens of the deep.

And yet right then – with the screaming in my ears and my vision dyed a blood red – I didn't care about how they looked or what they were. All that mattered to me was that they had been able to feel the glory of the beautiful cool water on their skin and I hadn't. They were actually dripping with the clear seawater, having such an abundance they let it fall around them. And I needed it too. Desired with everything I had to feel as they did, to be them.

Manacled there, Ludo and I were of no interest to this troupe of men from beneath the waves. They shambled past us as if we were of zero consequence, little more than driftwood.

Dead-eyed and on heavy limbs, they made their way undistracted into the village. Boots grinding on the shingle, but making no other sound. A silent brigade of drowned men moving past us.

Ludo and I strained with every atom of strength against our bonds, listened to the screaming in our heads and felt the burning of our skins. We watched those dead men go past and wished we could be like them, that we too could drown ourselves in the beautiful sea.

6. THE HORRORS OF BEDDNIC

Ludo Carstairs had dispensed with his sweat-stained shirt and sat on an old wooden chair, the flames from the hearth flickering shadows against his scrawny white torso. His hand trembling, he lifted a mug of room temperature whiskey to his chapped lips. It was nine-thirty the following morning and we were in Myfanwy's kitchen.

I couldn't manage to sit. Instead I was sprawled across the floor. A cold flannel draped over my forehead as if I had a fever. I cradled the same beverage Ludo had, although I hadn't yet brought myself to sip it.

His voice was weary and gravelly. He generally sounded older than his years, but now he could have lived millennia. "Tell us everything," he croaked. "You owe us that. How did all this begin?"

How we survived the night, or when each of us slipped into unconsciousness, I don't know. But in the morning, when the women came to free us, the hostility had melted away and been replaced with warm sympathy.

Myfanwy had looked at us almost maternally, or at least as if we were wayward puppies too pathetic to deserve a scolding.

It was she who answered.

"Six weeks ago." Her tone was admirably matter of fact. "Old man Pritchard took his customary evening stroll around the cliffs and never returned. Of course, we did that one proper. We called the police, the coastguard were alerted and we did everything we were supposed to do. Why would we do any different? Everyone knew that the old sod always had five pints in him before he went for his evening stroll, and that doing such a walk after dark was asking for trouble, even for a sober man. But he'd been a stubborn goat when young and there was simply no reasoning with him now. So, when he didn't come home that night, we thought we understood it. Obviously we'd never have wished *that* on him. We all wanted him found safe and sound, but we thought we understood what had happened.

"Even when his old body didn't wash up, when no glimmer of him could be found, we were confident that we understood."

An early morning rain shower was falling. The repeated taps on the window added accompaniment to her mournful tone.

"Corey Jenkins and Phil Hughes were next. Fishermen who went out on a clear morning and were never seen alive again. It was five days later and the sea really was so calm that day. It was like looking at smudged glass. You could have believed it was a picture of the sea, rather than the sea itself. Both of them were little more than boys. Jesus! Corey was only nineteen years old, he was a proper babe. Both of them had grown up on the water, they were so experienced with it. They should have come back. Even if there had been a horrendous storm, they should have had the innate skill to pull themselves home."

"Corey was my boyfriend." Beryl murmured. She sat on the floor beside me, her long legs curled in front of her, her arms crossed tight over her chest. "It wasn't serious. We weren't going to run away together or anything. But we had been boyfriend and girlfriend." She sighed deeply. "When he disappeared we weren't speaking. A stupid, silly argument. It made it much harder that he was gone. Infinitely harder."

Her left hand uncurled itself from being a shield around her, and reached out and stroked my hand. Since I'd been helped through the front door and then collapsed on this spot on the linoleum, she'd done that a couple of times. I thought it was to support me, to comfort me – but maybe it was the other way around.

"I remember those names," Ludo told them. "They were in the files we were given."

Myfanwy gave a single nod. "Again we called the police." She was the only one of the four of us standing. Telling the story while pottering around, pulling cups and plates off the draining board and putting them into the real wood cupboards. Sorting her kitchen as she talked because it obviously wasn't as ordered as it should have been. Perhaps it never was. "The local officers came and they were sympathetic and all. But there were odd looks and odd questions too. They could sense there was something else wrong. A deeper problem.

"Do you remember what happened years ago up the coast in Bridgend?"

I nodded, despite it hurting. "The suicides."

"For a while everyone thought that was a town full of freaks, and the same thing was happening to us."

"If I remember rightly," Ludo said, "the next to go were Thomas Lewis and Mark Weigh?"

"Correct," said Myfanwy.

"Thomas Lewis was my dad," Beryl said. "He'd left our house when I was a child, but he was still my dad."

"I'm very sorry," I murmured, making sure to clutch her fingers between mine.

"You called the police again," Ludo intoned. "I read the report and you were right, they were suspicious that something was going on here."

"And made no effort to hide their suspicions!" Myfanwy snapped.

"So after that you stopped calling?"

"It was our business," she said. "None of theirs. They didn't understand, couldn't understand. So what could they do to help us? Besides, this was something which only affected men. We could tell already that it was only the men of the town in any danger. And you can count the number of police women in this part of Wales on the fingers of a deformed hand. We thought it best not to involve any men from the outside. We thought it the better option to handle it ourselves."

Ludo said, "How quickly did it escalate after that?"

"Very quickly," Beryl told us. "All the men of the village were gone two days afterwards."

I was incredulous. "All of them?"

"Aye." Myfanwy nodded gravely. "Jasper Reynolds and Phil Vaughan made no secret of the fact they were heading inland, so we don't know what happened to them. We hope they escaped it. Pray they escaped it. The others, though they didn't go near the sea - even when they took pains to lock themselves in – they were still drawn to it. There was nothing we could do to stop them when the craving for the water came into their minds. One by one they walked unstoppable into the waves. Some ran, laughing and shouting crazy as they did.

"So what else could we do? We shut the road and tried to do our damndest to make sure that no other stupid men came in here and shared their fate." She sniffed. "It worked too, until you two idiots butted your noses in."

Ludo took a long sip from his mug. "Undeniably I feel an idiot, which – to be honest – is not a sensation I enjoy. Tell me, when did they start coming back?"

I shuddered, the dreadful images of what we'd seen last night flooding again though my mind.

"It was after Thomas and Mark. After Beryl's father went. But there were so few of them then that it seemed like something that wasn't real, as if they were ghosts."

Beryl interjected: "Mrs Rodgers said that she saw Mark and my dad staggering in the direction of the pub. She said that they already looked a dozen sheets to the wind."

"Old Mrs Rodgers' mind wanders." Myfanwy shook her head sadly. "I'm not sure she'd truly realised they were missing, so no one gave her any credence."

"Why would dad disappear for days on end and when he showed his face again, head straight to the pub? He wasn't the best of men and not the best of fathers, but he'd have known not to do that."

"Quite," said Ludo. "And what did they say at the pub? Did they see them?"

Beryl shook her head. "Teresa didn't see anything."

Taking another long draw from his mug, Ludo tried to sit straighter in the chair. I couldn't help but admire his stamina. It felt like my insides had been punched to a pulp. Despite obviously knowing that it would be good for me, that it would be fortifying, I hadn't taken a sip of my whiskey. I didn't yet have the stomach for it.

"But that's changed, hasn't it?" said Ludo. "One of my strongest memories from last night, as we lay there on the jagged blood-stained pebbles of the beach" (the two women shared a somewhat baffled glance at that) "was the men who came from the sea walking to the pub. My memory of last night falls shockingly far from total recall, but I think I saw them go in."

Myfanwy nodded. "They go in."

"What do they do?" I croaked. "They're not drinking, are they?"

"Ha!" Myfanwy snorted. "Do you think we'd leave a barmaid there to serve them? None of those bastards had any idea how to pull a pint when they were alive, they sure as hell don't whatever they are now."

"Carys Vaughan is reckless," Beryl's voice sunk low, sharing confidences. Possibly she was telling us something that Myfanwy herself didn't know. "She stole a peek through the window one night last week, she said they sit and stand around as they always did. They have no drinks in front of them and there didn't seem to be any conversation, they simply linger there. She said it was like they were waiting for something."

"Carys Vaughan is an idiot, that's what she is! A prize pudding!" Myfanwy slammed a casserole dish hard onto the counter.

"Do they all go in the pub?" I asked.

Beryl shook her head. "Some of them try to get back

into their old homes. They try the doors and rattle the windows and scream when they can't get them to open. There's a roar they make. It comes from low in their throats. It's a horrific noise, but it sounds like they're hurt, like they're crying because they can't get in."

"It's the same homes every night," Myfanwy whispered, her voice almost lost in the rataplan of falling rain. "We keep those ones empty, in case they do get in."

"What do you think they'd do if they did get through the door?" Ludo asked.

"We don't know in the slightest, Mr Carstairs," Myfanwy shook her head. "But we don't really want to learn that, do we?"

"But they haven't done anything yet, have they? They haven't hurt anybody yet?"

"No, they haven't! But we don't want to make it easy for them the day they do, do we?"

"They're zombies!" exclaimed Beryl, lost and overwhelmed by emotion. Her fingers tightened around mine.

"I apologise to you both." Ludo gave his best smile, which in the tired paleness of his face seemed unduly forced. "I didn't want it to appear I was challenging you. I just wanted to establish exactly where we are now."

Myfanwy's hands went to her hips as she stood over him. "We've had every damn man in this village lured into the water. Seemingly to their deaths. But they're emerging from the water, walking corpses, night after night. Their skin decomposed by the tides and eaten by the bloody fish. That's where we are right now, Mr Carstairs. That's where we are!"

He took a final thoughtful sip. "My friend, Garris

met a genuine zombie in the Caribbean a few years ago, didn't you, Garris?"

"That wasn't this!" I mumbled, wanting to shut him up quickly.

"No, from what I've seen, this is something completely different. As here we have the added variable of the HMS Mandrake, sunk out there in the deep with its radio suddenly transmitting."

"What?" Beryl and Myfanwy's voices rose at once.

"Whatever is going on here," Ludo told them, "it is much bigger than Beddnic."

7. WATCHING LUDO WORK

I sat on a low stone wall right at the edge of the beach, about fifteen foot or so from the metal pole we'd been chained to last night. Ludo paced back and fore across the beach, crunching the pebbles and tramping a groove into the shingle. His over shirt was on again, but his sleeves were rolled up. I'd seen it before. The pondering, the prevarication, the self-doubt. In the crisp morning air he looked agonised, but it wouldn't last long. Decisive action was more Ludo's style.

The rain clouds had blown away and the day had become one of picturesque cold blue horizons, offering vistas to the sky and sea which showed this village to be a wonderful place of seclusion. Seeing it that way almost expunged the blood-soaked images from my mind. Instead I enjoyed the morning's calmness in the lovely cove, with the breath-taking views and the phenomenally clean air. The only thing I'd seen more beautiful recently was Beryl.

Maybe I blushed as she approached me, worried that she might have a low level psionic ability and be able to read my thoughts. It was a relief then that the tired but genuine smile on her face didn't suggest any embarrassment.

She walked straight to my side, her hair long and straight over her shoulders – as if she'd recently taken the time to brush it. Her skin was luminous in the sunlight.

"Hi," she said.

I stood up. "Hello."

If the tide ever got high enough, I guessed the wall I'd been sitting on would be a bit of a breaker. Although if it ever came in that strong, I'm not sure the old stone bricks would last. I wasn't interested right then in aged walls, however.

Beryl's face was marred by puzzlement.

She said, "What did your friend mean when he said you saw a zombie?"

I sighed. Despite being privately employed, we were signatories of onerous Official Secrets Acts for a variety countries. Ludo Carstairs however, saw them as ridiculous bits of paper. Details he could choose to ignore.

"That was on St Lucia," I told her. "Zombies there aren't similar to the ones you see in the films. That type of zombie isn't real. What I saw, what I dealt with, is more a dark art form. It's one person taking control of another's will and it isn't pleasant."

She nodded once, her front teeth biting into her bottom lip as she tried to take this new world in. "So there was a person behind this zombie? A bad guy?"

"A real bastard."

"And did you catch him? Stop him?"

"How do you know it was a he?"

"It's always a man who does stuff like that."

I stared away from her eager eyes and over the beach, not particularly wanting to remember my Caribbean adventure in too great a detail. "We got the victim healthy again, in their own mind. That was the important thing."

After only a fraction of hesitation, Beryl sat on the wall. I then sat back down beside her. She followed my gaze. Fixing her eyes on Ludo and watching transfixed as he paced relentlessly: a human metronome. No, his movements weren't actually smooth enough for that, he was more a zig-zag of nerves. I thought I could see him talking to himself.

"Is he the one who'll solve this?" she asked. "Will he work out what we have to do to stop it?"

"He'll try."

"So, he's the bright one and you're the compassionate one?"

A grin creased my mouth and moved my cheeks. Amazing, given that my face ached as much as the rest of me. "Are you impugning my intelligence, Beryl?"

"Oh my God!" Her hand clutched my arm as she laughed, her cheeks flushing an attractive red. I'd never heard her laugh before. It was like listening to the loveliest choral music ever composed. "I didn't mean that! It's just that he's really smart, isn't he?"

"He's a genius."

"But he's not very good with normal people?"

"A lot of geniuses aren't."

"And so I was wondering how the dynamic between the two of you worked." She blushed again. "I'm sorry, I didn't mean anything by it. Really I didn't."

I smiled reassuringly. "He's the best of us. Of all of us who work together, he is the number one and everyone knows that. I'm pretty good myself, but maybe you have hit upon the reason why we're partnered. I'm friendlier than him. I don't end up treating whatever is in front of me as an academic exercise. I care more about the damage I might cause."

We watched him pace. Every ten yards or so he'd swivel around on his hip and then pound the other way. Undoubtedly he'd be aware that the two of us were staring at him, but he wouldn't care.

"So will he solve it all then?" she asked. "Will he manage to get my dad back? Jason back? Everybody else?"

I hesitated. "I don't know if this is St Lucia, Beryl. I don't know if we'll be able to get them back again. Back the way they were before."

"But they come here each night, Mr Garris?"

"Something does. We don't really know that it's them."

"But they go to the pub." The emotion was rising in her voice. "They try to go home, to do the things they used to do. There has to be something of them left there, there just has to be."

She grabbed my hand, holding it tight between smooth, beautiful – if icy cold – fingers.

"I know you're trying to be gentle with me, Mr Garris. You're trying to stop me getting too hopeful. I understand that. But what I really need right now is blind foolish hope. Some idiotic bloody optimism! That's what I need. Will you let me have that, Mr Garris? Will you?" Beryl stared at Ludo again, before turning her pleading, deep brown eyes to me. "Will he make things right?"

"He'll do his best." I squeezed her fingers in mine.

8. LUDO'S PLAN

"I've radioed The Chief," Ludo told us finally. "I've asked for a conversation, a discourse as it were."

"With The Chief?" I asked.

"No, with whatever it is that's lying there in the deep."

Beryl and Myfanwy stared at him open-mouthed. We were in Myfanwy's kitchen again. The kettle was on and a large, recently defrosted, home-made apple pie sat on the table. Myfanwy had given it twenty minutes in the oven and it smelled delicious. It occurred to me that I hadn't eaten in about twenty-four hours. Still, I resisted taking the first slice – both out of politeness and because the moment didn't seem right. The moment rarely seemed right when Ludo was on the charge. He was a man who subsisted on air and adrenaline.

Myfanwy's eyes narrowed "What do you mean, whatever is there?"

"The HMS Mandrake is a sunken wreck lying only a couple of miles from here," Ludo stated. "As I understand it, it was a type of experimental communications ship, which despite its seabed residence would now seem to be broadcasting two signals. One is the standard SOS, which has – for reasons unknown – switched itself on for the first time in seventy years, while the other is… Well, I'll be honest with you, I'm not quite sure what the other is. None of us are. But it doesn't take many leaps of logic to surmise that it's responsible for what's going on here."

With both women's eyes on him, Ludo leant across the table and cut a good sized piece of apple pie and put it in his bowl. He then poured the custard from the earthenware jug next to it. A tuckshop grin on his face, he raised the bowl in compliments to the chef and then passed it wordlessly to me.

I blushed a little that he could read me so well, but wasn't going to resist it.

"I'm lost." Myfanwy's face was the embodiment of disdain. "This might all be making sense to you and your big brain, Mr Carstairs, but us mere mortals haven't got a clue what the bloody hell you're talking about. Tell us again, what have you done and what are you planning on doing?"

He sat back on the old chair. "I have had a signal sent. The SOS is set out in old British Naval code, so I've responded with a message in the same code asking for a conversation."

"But how is responding to the SOS going to make any difference?" Beryl asked. "You said it was the other signal that was causing the problems. Do you understand this, Mr Garris?"

"I think so." I stared hard at Ludo, wondering if the day would ever come when he'd consult me on one of his plans before he enacted it. "He's hoping there's an intelligence in the water. Something which awoke recently and switched on those messages. An unknown something which is – presumably – listening to them. And he's hoping that this intelligent something will pick up his signal, understand what it means, and respond."

"I'm hoping," Ludo said, clearly pleased with himself, "that tonight it will send one of the men of Beddnic to speak to us."

Myfanwy took a step towards him, outraged. "Are you telling me that rather than getting rid of these things from our nightmares, you've invited one of them here to chew the fat?"

"But it could tell us what's going on," Beryl spoke quickly, "it could tell us how to stop this. How to get them back properly."

"Don't you believe it, my girl. It will tell us what Mr Carstairs wants to hear. He's not interested in stopping it, he only wants to know how it works."

"I do want to stop this, Myfanwy," he told her earnestly. "That's my intention. I promise you that."

"We will stop this!" I assured them. Although maybe I would have sold the sentiment better if I didn't already have a big spoonful of apple pie into my mouth.

"And what do you imagine we'll do?" Myfanwy's temper was rising to boiling point. She was glaring at both of us. "When the body of a man we knew, someone we loved, walks in here and asks us for a bit of a chat? Talk to him about the fishing this year, or the rugby, or what he'd want for bloody Christmas? Aren't you forgetting that you won't be here when they come to visit us tonight? Or at least not in any way that they'll be able to get sense from you, or you get sense from them."

"I haven't forgotten that at all." Ludo smiled. "But I think I might have a work around."

"A work around!" she scoffed. "What's that then?"

"We'll be shackled indoors tonight, underground. There must be a basement we can use somewhere in this village. Hopefully that will deaden most of the effect, although I know that we'll be vulnerable."

Myfanwy scowled at him. "Oh, that's good to hear. It's nice to know you've determined a way for you to be okay. And what do we do in the meantime then? Act as a welcoming committee? Hang bunting?"

"They never hurt the women of this village," Ludo intoned. "Come on, we've all noticed that. You say they try to break into houses – their former homes – but they never go after the people they left behind. They have never ever hurt you women. And I'm betting that will stay the case tonight. I'm not asking any of you to get too near them, but if a few – maybe, the reckless Carys Vaughan, for instance – could lead them our way, that would be much appreciated."

"Are you sure about this?" I asked.

"Pretty much," he told us. "It's not a perfect plan, but we don't have much daylight and time is pressing."

Myfanwy glared at him. "I hate men with confidence as cheap as their aftershave, Mr Carstairs. There better be value in yours!"

With that she stormed out of her own home.

9. THE SECOND NIGHT

No doubt the autodidact in Ludo had enough rudimentary knowledge of Welsh home design of the 1930s to know that most of these houses would have basements before he formulated his plan. We had a wide choice and were able to find a basement in the first row of houses from the beach which was pleasantly furnished. There was an old oak table (which may have been older than the house), chairs of a similar vintage and a whole set of metal shelves filled with jars of pickled fruit and vegetables.

Most importantly, from our point of view, it had a horizontal metal bar cemented into the wall about halfway up. The only sensible purpose we could think of for it, was for a man to pull himself to safety if he was trapped there while the basement was flooding. The other possible use was to chain up strangers.

Maybe it was genuinely the latter. The house belonged to a Mrs Gertrude Hannah, who apparently didn't seem surprised or nonplussed when Beryl told her that the two strange Englishmen in town wanted to chain themselves in her basement. But then, these women were at the point where they'd accept any mild strangeness to remove the dreadful strangeness each evening wrought.

"My theory is that to survive this night we have to dull our senses," Ludo told me cheerfully. A good humour which felt more than a little forced.

We sat at the table, the chain of the manacles was wrapped once around the table legs and then hooked through that strange iron bar on the wall. The manacles themselves were chained again over our wrists. My left wrist was aching and chafed, and there was – I admit – a second of panic at being confined once more, but I wore my best stoic expression as Myfanwy and Beryl snapped the restraint shut.

There was no situation though in which Ludo Carstairs couldn't make himself sound charmingly chipper. "If we can dull our senses, put a whole solid house of brick and stone between us and the eerie call of the sea, then hopefully we'll be able to function. Can you hear the waves?"

There was always a fresh surprise with Ludo. Today's had been him reaching into his pockets and pulling out a small green plastic case, inside which were two sets of luminous yellow rubber earplugs. Why he would ever have thought he'd need such things, I don't know. When I asked, he simply smiled and told me he was always prepared. If he wasn't such a born insubordinate, I could have believed that he'd been King of the Scouts.

The earplugs in place, I shook my head. "No, I can't!"

It meant we had to speak loudly to each other, virtually yell, but it also meant that we couldn't hear the sea. Obviously in the basement we couldn't see it either.

The salt air guaranteed though that we couldn't avoid the fact it was nearby.

"How much of your new theory is hunch based, and how much is based on facts that you think I haven't noticed?" I asked him.

He grinned. "Oh, it's pretty much all hunch based. But come, Garris, you of all people know how good my hunches can be."

"One day you're going to get one very wrong, Ludo."

"And when I do, I'm sure you or someone of your ilk will be there to point it out. Until then, let's hope that whatever's there has received and understood our message. It's going to be a long and painful evening otherwise."

It was an incredibly long and painful evening anyway.

Despite the basement, despite the earplugs and the dulling of our senses, it was a tortuously drawn out night.

Although we couldn't see it, sunset hit us both hard.

It was a sharp pricking of the skin first of all. The cold spokes of a thousand metal combs pressing their points into every inch of my body. Creating an itch that was both all-encompassing and yet impossible to reach. Swiftly my skin was burning, as if it was red raw and covered with flaming ants.

The only good thing right then was the smell of the sea. It played on my nostrils. Tempted me. Whispered to me that there was a place with no pain. If I went to the sea that would stop my suffering, it would soothe my skin, it would make absolutely everything better. I had to get to the sea.

My memory is cloaked in dreadful shadow, but I can remember turning my head and staring at the heavy basement door above us. Maybe I tried to throw myself from my seat in its direction, to yank at my restraints.

Ludo snapped his left hand over my wrist. Squeezing and twisting at my skin.

As if in a daze, slowly and drunkenly I stared in his direction. For the last few moments, I'd actually forgotten he was there.

"You've got to concentrate, Garris!" His voice was both urgent and desperate, and yet faint and far away. "Concentrate on something other than your physical sensations. Don't let them overwhelm you, don't acknowledge them. Look at this table, for instance. Someone spent many hours labouring over this table. A proper artisan who took pride in his work. How old do you think this table is? A hundred years? More, perhaps? How many people do you think have sat around it? In all these years, how many? Think of all the stories they must have told. Think of all the wonderful tales which must have happened right at this table. All the love stories begun and all the love stories ended right here.

"You don't get tables remotely close to this anymore, Garris, you really don't. Most tables you sit at these days are mass produced crap. Warehouse crap. They really are. But this one – it's amazing, Garris. There is a wealth of history right in front of us. Do you think it's reclaimed wood? If so, that would stretch its history to a date much further back, give it many more tales to tell. Think of the table, Garris, focus your mind and think of what's in front of you."

My vision was floating, but I looked at Ludo as he

stared at that damn table. It was as if every single grain within the wood fascinated and transfixed him. With my heart racing and my muscles desperate to get away, I tried my best to follow his lead. But I couldn't. It was too hard. My skin was burning and I could feel the sweat stinging into my eyeballs.

Still he clutched my wrist tight. "You have to concentrate, Garris. Please concentrate."

By now it must be fully dark outside; I could sense that even as I had no idea what time it was. Every heartbeat felt an eternity. I was suffering, the darkness was going to consume me whole, and the only thing which could offer any relief was the blessed, beautiful sea.

I think I made another fevered lurch towards the door, the manacle digging deeper into my skin.

"From where do you hail, Garris?" Ludo demanded, his hand clinging onto me.

He knew perfectly well where I was from, but I understood what he was doing.

Still though, my tongue felt too fat in my mouth, swollen and impossible to use.

"Where do you call home?" he practically yelled.

"Dorking," I managed to reply, although the name sounded garbled to my ears.

"Where did you go to school?"

"St Bartholomew's."

"Then where?"

I stared longingly towards the door. "Durham," I managed finally.

"You have to keep concentrating, Garris! Focus and keep your wits about you. It's so tempting to throw it in, I realise that, but you have to try!"

His words seemed virtually meaningless to me. I

couldn't see how I could focus, couldn't imagine right then keeping hold of my own mind.

It was impossible!

I couldn't hear the waves or see the sea, but I could feel its pull. It was in every one of my bones, tugging at them all.

Ludo scrunched his face tight and practically bellowed into my ear. "Concentrate!"

And then the door above us swung open and gave us something that we had no choice but to concentrate on.

10. THE EMISSARY FROM THE DEEP

Beryl told us later that it was easy to recognise which of the men who returned to Beddnic every night had been sent ashore this evening for a conversation.

All the others – those decaying wrecks who used to be men – were stumbling and aimless. It broke her heart to look at them, to properly see them. They resembled little more than braindead zombies.

Except for one.

Even in the clouded darkness, it was obvious who he was. While the others slipped and staggered around him, he stood still. Feet planted on the tarmac pathway from the beach, his oddly bright eyes staring about furiously.

In life his name had been Jason Jenkins and he had been one of the last to be taken. He was a young man, twenty-five, tall and muscular with long straight black hair which fell to his shoulders. While alive he'd worked for The Forestry Service and had driven from Beddnic to work each morning. Right until the day he didn't.

When I asked Beryl about him much later, she blushed. I don't know if that meant the most beautiful girl in the village and surely a strong contender for the most handsome bloke ever had a fling, or whether she merely had a crush on him. She's never said.

That night, she told me, he looked like something from *The Night of the Living Dead*. His skin was deathly pale, with blue veins telegraphed from his neck to his forehead. The once cared for mane had grown long and hung straggly halfway down his spine, while his fingernails were sharp points and grubby – as if he used them to tear out the innards of passing fish. Most disturbing were the eyes. She said in that eerily white face, it was like there was a dark fire to them.

It was the young girls who took the lead. The ones who could run fastest. Scared well beyond their years, they were still happy to help in any way they could.

When Jenkins stopped at the head of the beach, when he made his presence known, it was reckless Carys Vaughan who ran out first. Scarpering on plimsolls, she gave a throaty cry that he should follow. Then, when he was nearer the houses, Carys ducked away, and the much younger Gemma Evans dashed forward and led him onto the right street. Finally, it was Beryl herself who caught his attention, yelling and whooping from the darkness, but doing enough to bring him through Mrs Hannah's front door.

He was fast, she said. Despite the sodden deadness of his limbs, he was quick. Not quite mobile enough on his feet to actually catch three daring but terrified girls, yet – she said – the intentness of his eyes showed that he wouldn't surrender. As if he knew they'd eventually tire, while he never would.

Once in the house, Beryl ducked upstairs and it was Myfanwy who lured him to the basement. With a harsh rhythm, she banged a ladle into a metal saucepan in the darkness of the kitchen. Then she watched him through the doorway and over the floor as he came closer and closer.

His lack of true nimbleness didn't matter much anymore in the confines of that kitchen. If he wanted to, he could come for her and she'd have no way to squeeze past.

Breathless, Myfanwy swung open that heavy basement door and stepped into the shadows – hoping that Ludo was right and he'd take the bait. The basement light was on – the one light in the village still illuminated – so when he came into the kitchen it was the obvious destination. But who knew what went through this creature's mind? What was obvious to him?

Having got his attention, Myfanwy now cowered silent and hidden in a dark far corner of the kitchen and hoped that he'd already forgotten about her.

There was a moment, apparently, when he paused. When his mouth opened and closed and his eyes – shining with their weird dark light – fixed straight on her. Maybe he wanted to take something up with her; to make whatever demands he had of her – as if he knew that she was the real de facto leader of Beddnic. His hesitation lasted only a heartbeat, but Myfanwy – unyielding and stoic Myfanwy – nearly screamed. He was three steps away and she knew that she had nowhere to go and nothing with which to protect herself. So she was ready to scream; a scream that would no doubt have contained a curse on the soul of Ludo Carstairs.

But then, Jason Jenkins – or the thing that had once been Jason Jenkins – turned his neck slowly (the muscles of his neck seemingly creaking) and stared towards the solitary light. He took three plodding, yet determined steps forward.

Myfanwy only moved again when he stepped into the light, and then – with a gasp something like relief – she slammed the basement door behind him.

11. IN THE BASEMENT WITH A DEAD MAN

The door slammed. Open-mouthed, we both stared at the new arrival. A dead man who shimmered blue.

I felt Ludo's fingernails dig sharp into my skin, telling me I had to focus. Now of all times, I couldn't let myself get distracted. I had to be in control.

But in my mind, I could suddenly hear the waves. The sound of them lapping at the shore was mesmerising. It was real and beautiful to me. So much so, that when I stared at this new arrival – a man from the depths – I thought he must be a friend. More than that, it seemed there was an instant fraternal bond between us.

Looking back, that feeling is unfathomable to me. The moisture on his skin sparkled and I wanted to feel that same water on me. But when I think of him standing there – dead and pale and starting to rot – I know there was nothing about the way he looked that should have provoked such feelings of admiration.

And yet I loved him, wanted to be at his side

wherever he went.

His skin was swollen a sickly grey, the top layer of epidermis flaking off. I can remember his lips puffed out and green, as if his very blood was now seaweed and saltwater. There were thick veins stretching from his mouth – lines blue and turquoise. They resembled a map, a guide to a forgotten and forbidden land stencilled right there on this man's face. Or what used to be a man. He was a form of aquatic evolution, a creature who had started homo-sapiens, but now lived below the waves to become something much, much more.

In slow response to the door slamming behind him, he stared around, bafflement on his face. His resiliently muscular shoulders slumped towards the door, making a weak attempt to force it open. But then his gaze fixed on us sat at the bottom of the stairs. His eyes had once been dark brown, but the colour was faded and there was something else – darker, crueller, not remotely human – caught within them.

Even today, I can't decide how much actual life I perceived in those eyes. There was a spark of intelligence, certainly, but it didn't belong to man. Or really to any creature that we recognise as alive on this planet. The glow within those orbs was something different; uncanny and indescribable.

"Focus, Garris!" Ludo hissed.

"I'm trying!" I just about muttered.

I was trying, but it was dreadfully hard. There was a quality so attractive about this man – about this creature – who had come in to join us. My higher mind could see there was nothing but decay and darkness to him, and yet I was drawn to his presence. It wasn't like I wanted to be with this thing that used to be a man.

No, instead I wanted to *be* him. Desperately, I wanted to be a creature of the water too.

A million voices hissed and prompted at my ears. Beseeching me, pushing me forward. The sound of the sea was so magnificently loud and enticing. It was horrible and yet wonderful. My whole being was a spinning tumult of emotions and sensations, a constant scream which felt without end. There would be no peace until I reached the water. The beautiful, blessed sea.

I tried not to cry to the unseen stars and lose myself completely. All I could do was concentrate on Ludo's unrelenting nails. I was straining at my manacles, while at the same time he tore his fingers into my skin.

Slowly and agonisingly, I turned my gaze and stared straight at Ludo's face. Trying to draw strength from him.

I could see it in Ludo's eyes and in the redness of his skin, the sheer mental effort he was exerting. How every sinew of him was determined not to be overwhelmed. His jaw was locked firm and he was clearly biting into the insides of his cheeks – there were thin trails of blood dribbling from between his clenched lips and over his jaw. What I really focused on however was his forehead. There was a thin vein beating furiously from his hairline to his brow: his big brain behind doing all it could to maintain control.

The sight of him steeled me, gave me the wit to tap into my own reserves. His fingers squeezed into my skin and I knew I had to return the favour. As his hand clutched mine, I grabbed his arm and twisted the bare flesh in an old schoolroom burn. The wince of pain on his face was followed by a small, grateful, weary smile.

Behind me the creature had made its way, clumsy

and sodden – yet holding itself upright – down the wooden steps. Now it stared at us, perhaps trying to determine which one was in charge.

Everything about it called to me. As I turned, I could smell the sea reeking deliciously from it, see the wondrous life-giving water pooling tantalisingly beneath it on the stone floor.

Once again I twisted Ludo's skin as he dug into mine.

Slowly, Ludo met the creature's gaze and raised his free hand. A greeting and an acknowledgement of authority.

Its dark eyes were staring at us and we were staring at it. Lord knows how long we could go on before we weakened and broke; before we tried to smash our manacles and embrace this creature; let it take us to the exalted peace of underwater.

Silence wasn't good. We had to break this impasse.

Fortunately, Ludo's raised hand seemed to be the signal the creature needed.

Suddenly its arm shot to its forehead, in a clumsy but clearly sincere military salute.

"What are our orders?" it asked in a gravelly, yet clipped English accent.

12. 'WHAT ARE OUR ORDERS?'

"Orders?" Ludo's voice was a little high, but that was the only sign of the physical torment he endured. "What do you mean? Orders?"

Its accent was unmistakable, but despite looking and moving like a man, there was a deadness to the voice it used. It was a voice that belonged to someone else entirely, *something* else entirely. A gravelly whisper dragged across the soil of a graveyard. Its breath – though I might have hallucinated this – had the whiff of sulphur.

It said, "The orders we need. The reconnaissance is complete. We need orders for the next stage of the operation."

From the corner of my eye, I saw Ludo jerk his head. The waves continued to crash over and through my consciousness, yet he was somehow pushing himself above it. There was a stillness to him, but he must have been paddling furiously.

"What's your name, soldier?" Ludo barked.

The creature stared at us blankly for few seconds,

the light seeming to fade from its eyes.

"Your name?" Ludo snapped again. "Rank? Service number? Come, I can't be expected to provide you with pertinent orders if I don't know whom I'm dealing with!"

Within the creature's eyes, the light seemed to flare bright again. "Names are unimportant in this operation. We are the Army of the Deep."

I can remember a shudder passing through me. It was the final word which did it. The creature drew it out in that decayed voice so that it resembled a curse.

In my head, the cry of the voices and the crashing of the waves became more intense. They were echoing this creature's voice, demonstrating that it was not alone, that it was part of something larger.

Beside me, I felt Ludo give an involuntary tremble. Even with all his fortitude, he couldn't make himself immune. My hand twisted harder against his skin and, somehow, he managed to retain his composure.

"But you must have a name, soldier, you must have an identity!"

Again, whatever that intelligence was seemed to slip into the depths of the creature's eyeballs. It never blinked, not once while it was with us, but the light in its eyes ebbed and flowed.

"Identities are unimportant." It told us finally. "*We* are the one. *We* are the Army of the Deep."

"One for all and all for one," Ludo muttered. "Although, I suppose it doesn't really matter if one of you doesn't come back – the perfect fighting force."

The creature, stood at the head of the table, leant forward on its toes. Perhaps hoping that Ludo would provide the orders it needed.

"You mentioned reconnaissance," Ludo said.

"What have you discovered on this reconnaissance?"

"This town is harmless. It is not a strategic target."

"Harmless?"

"No weapons, no soldiers, nothing of military interest." Its voice didn't sound like it came from a man, but equally it sounded straight out of Sandhurst. "The first phase was completed and remaining there are only the women. No opposition reinforcements have been dispatched."

Ludo swallowed before speaking. "Women?" his voice croaked. He shook his head, trying everything he could to keep his mind clear. "Who are these women, soldier?"

"The women are us."

"*Us*. Like the *we*?"

There was a pause and the creature swayed back on its heels, the light flickering in its eyes.

"You said names weren't important and you were a collective 'we'," Ludo tried again. "Is that the same for 'us'? Are these women connected to you, soldier?"

I could feel the blood from my wrist trickling onto the table, pooling under my arm. When he spoke, the blood from Ludo's lip speckled as well.

If only we could cleanse ourselves in the sparkling water which dripped from that creature's clothes.

"They are who we are fighting for. They are us," the creature told us finally, as if it was the definitive answer. "King and country!"

Ludo nodded, trying to stay calm as his eyeballs bulged in pain. "You've been on reconnaissance, haven't you, soldier? You've found yourselves away from the fight and, having concluded that this town is harmless, you don't know what to do with yourselves. You need orders to go into battle. That's the second phase."

The answer came quickly, with maybe an air of relief. "Yes."

"Come here, soldier!" Ludo ordered.

The creature stared at him.

"I gave you an order, soldier."

Its expression blank but dutiful, the creature marched around the table from me. With its limbs loose and shuffling, it still maintained a military air. The muscles of the body might have begun rotting, but there was more than enough present for it to be formidable in combat.

Actually trying a wet and uncoordinated stamp of the heel, the creature presented itself right in front of Ludo. It was a good soldier who understood the importance of hierarchy, it merely wanted to receive its orders.

Even now, I'm not quite sure how Ludo did what he did one-handed. With his right hand clinging onto me (and my hand still clinging onto him), he somehow reached into his pocket and whipped out a pair of handcuffs. Then, in a little less than a blink of the eye, one cuff was snapped tight around that creature's wrist, with the other thrown over the metal bar in the wall.

"Here's your order!" Ludo said. "You're to stay here with us!"

13. THE FURIOUS PRISONER

It howled.

That's the only way I can describe the sound it made. Although that word in no way does justice to the excruciating, dreadful cacophony which emanated from that creature's dead lips. It was brutal pain given its own song. A wailing, drawn-out noise; a choir of the tortured – each of them going through the most diabolic torments and made to scream in unison. It was decades of pent-up suffering unleashed in one nearly endless cry. I dread to think how unbearable the sound would have been if we had not worn earplugs.

When it stood at the table, I'd thought it was weakening. It swayed on its feet and I surmised whatever connection had tethered it to the deep was flickering. But the instant Ludo snapped the cold steel handcuff around that wrist, its shoulders rose and it seemed to have a rejuvenated power channelling through it.

Its palms open, its dead and overgrown fingernails bared, it lashed at Ludo. Those dark, dirty claws swiped through the air millimetres in front of Ludo's face. They were talons, death and water having sharpened them to animalistic claws. Ludo fell as the creature lurched desperately over the table and tried to slice his throat. No longer regarding him as a potential commanding officer; recognising him absolutely as the enemy.

The manacles around our wrists trapped us almost as effectively as the handcuff trapped it, but Ludo was ready. He'd known what his plan was all along.

Dropping his knees to the floor, he shoved with all the strength of his shoulders and pushed the table over. Heavy and aged oak that it was, he managed to smash it onto its side. The chain binding us slipped off the table leg and gave us more room to wriggle. Together we pushed the table towards the creature and then shuffled backwards ourselves, getting as far away as we could.

It grabbed at us, it swiped at us, but all on its own it wasn't actually strong enough to resist as we forced the table into its midriff and stumbled it on its heels into the stone wall. Its free arm lashing into Mrs Hannah's shelves. A dozen jars of pickled produce dropping and smashing on the solid floor.

Breathless I stared. Its cries becoming pitiful even as they roared angrily. There were no words anymore, only shapeless fury. The dampness of its skin flared blue, making it appear less like a man – instead it was a carnivorous fish on rotting limbs. Despite that, it was impossible for me not to notice the beautiful way it shimmered. Obviously I knew we had to trap it, that I was helping Ludo, but a huge part of me wanted to be with the creature.

"Garris!" barked Ludo.

Clearly the creature no longer saw me as a potential ally either and I ducked away fast enough to see the sharpened points of its fingers flash before my eyeballs. I'd been gawping at it, and it had nearly taken my naïve, awestruck face off.

We shuffled further away, as far as the chain would allow. The creature handcuffed to the wall couldn't get to us, but just as we'd used the table against it, it could use it against us. We braced ourselves on the floor and pushed our feet against the underside of the aged oak. Making sure that this thing which was once named Jason Jenkins couldn't make a move.

Still howling and with pain so obviously tormenting every inch of it, it swiped at us. But it didn't have the mobility or flexibility to get near our ankles. Its eyes were burning. What had been flickering embers of intelligence was now a cauldron of fury. It foamed at the lips. Dried, fleshy spittle bubbling from its mouth and dripping a dull brown onto the stone floor. The smell was salt water mixed with putrid meat. The deliciousness of the first mitigated by the awfulness of the second. As well as its skin decaying, the creature was clearly rotting on the inside.

My wrist aching, my own blood dripping to the floor, I managed to hold my mind together and glare at the creature we'd cornered. Its eyes burned and its jaw contorted, but it was also helpless. Whatever actually constituted its intelligence had clearly never gone through a learning process that would enable it to climb over the table. It had no capacity to reason its way out of this predicament.

Still – despite how much it repulsed me – I wanted to be it. The waves were in my mind, no matter how much I didn't want to think of them. I shook my head and concentrated. It was my turn to bite hard on the inside of my cheeks. Pain was the only thing which made me feel like me.

From above us, there was a sudden hammering like thunder.

The heavy door to the basement was being rattled angrily by possibly a dozen fists.

Staring towards the racket, staring at the creature, I realised that I'd heard distant cries of warning. Not human voices, not words – instead threatening whispers that came on the ever closer waves. They were telling me (telling us, as Ludo confirmed later that he'd heard them too) that the Army of the Deep was coming for us. That we needed to surrender. They were telling us that we should throw ourselves into the sea.

The smashing hands on the wood, the crashing waves – both were warnings. They told us we were wrong to resist; that there was no escape. Without surrender, there would be only dreadful punishment.

My senses reeling, I nearly lost consciousness. The noise, the pain: everything was overwhelming. My eyes rolled and my legs nearly buckled against the table. Still the creature thrashed at it, claws and spittle flying. As I weakened, as it all became too much, I nearly pitched forward and presented my neck to it.

"Hold the course, Garris!" Ludo yelled. "We have to hold the course!"

I jerked back. Every inch of me ached. My head pounded and my ears rang. But the firm reassurance of Ludo's words also beat remorselessly into my skull. It was there with the sounds of the sea, the banging of the door, the millions of voices crying at me with rage, while others offered temptation.

If I gave in, my life would be one of peacefulness. I

knew that as certainly as I knew rain fell from the sky. It would be lovely to let the creature have what it wanted. To submit, to follow it and sink away into the blessed water.

My gaze met Ludo's piercing blue eyes, reserves of strength passing between us. I wasn't going to quit. No matter how much I wanted to, I was not going to wrestle Ludo for the handcuffs' key and give the creature its freedom. That wasn't who I was. That wasn't my duty.

The creature seemed to dislocate its wrist in the handcuff, to almost separate its hand from its body. With a crunch of bone and an eldritch cry, it lurched towards us, scratching the table across the floor in our direction. Buckling at the waist, so it was nearly toppling over the top, it swung down and tried to slice Ludo's feet apart.

Ludo yelped in surprise. Then he straightened his legs again. We both did. Doing our best to ignore our own strength failing. Obviously there was no way we could do this for much longer, yet we had to try.

It roared in front of us. The thing cried from low in its throat, a gurgle which sounded neither man nor animal – it was the deep and the dead and all matter of darkness wrapped into a terrifying primal scream. A noise so horrendous it seemed to shake those solid walls.

Above us the fists banged more furiously, managing to shake the hinges. As sturdy as that door was, it wasn't going to resist forever.

Ludo and I glanced at each other. Our legs locked straight, we cried as one. A roar of determination to disguise our fear.

But then – apart from our own cry – the noise was

gone. The banging slipped back to a few isolated, feeble slaps. There were no longer many fists smashing against the door in fury. Instead, the sound was unmistakably akin to surrendering.

In my ears, the crashing of the waves subsided. It faded away, as if – in that basement – it had never really been there at all.

And for perhaps half a minute or so, as the creature stared with bulging eyes at us, there was peaceful silence.

It was as quiet as being in a room with an actual dead man.

But then there came a scream.

No, multiplied.

Screams.

An agonising rage which erupted from the creature's mouth, but seemed to belong to many voices simultaneously. A noise that was cruelly symphonic and consumed everything else around it. The glass jars which hadn't already perished, burst apart at that scream.

My eyes squeezed shut and I raised my hands to my ears and thought that I was drowning. Being overwhelmed not by water, but tormenting sound. A cry so encompassing, it was going to flood my senses and destroy everything of me. It was rampaging through my brain, determined to utterly crush my spirit and rip apart my soul. What good were earplugs when confronted with this implacable resonance?

I felt Ludo shaking beside me, convulsing almost. Our bodies contorted by the same piercing pain. My arms reached to him, the belief certain that this trip to Beddnic was the mission which finally ended us.

The creature's pale face loomed into us and it

roared. That roar came from the vast expanse of the sea.

But then it eased.

Then it stopped.

The screaming went first. Subsiding in my mind to a distant, mournful whisper and then nothing.

After that, the creature, which had seemed full of unquenchable fury, crumpled to its knees in front of us. Its whole body slumping at once, until its face smacked limply – and with a moist splat – against the stone floor

Ludo and I clung to each other. Panting, dripping with sweat, each of us trying to put the fragments of our minds together again.

"I think," Ludo croaked eventually, "morning has broken."

14. DAWN

"They're not your loved ones." Mug of whiskey again in hand, Ludo was bluntness itself.

We were still in Mrs Hannah's cellar. Myfanwy and Beryl having joined us with a bottle of Irish strength.

Beryl was on her knees, stroking through the lank damp hair of the man who had lived his life as Jason Jenkins. Before he came back as something else altogether. Myfanwy stared at us and then at Beryl with her cheeks sunk in and her skin ashen. The bags under her eyes were marble gravestone black.

"They've taken their bodies. They have trampled their souls. Your souls as well. But, they are not your loved ones. Not anymore. They haven't been since they took their last mortal breaths."

"What are they then?" Myfanwy asked quietly.

Ludo and I had un-manacled ourselves. Again the night's exertions seemed to have taken a greater toll on me and I was crumpled in the corner, a fresh white bandage wrapped around my arm. It was the only thing about me which seemed clean. The material of my shirt was stuck to my skin with sweat, while blood stained my sleeves and trousers.

"They're an army of corpses. They describe themselves as the Army of the Deep, and that is exactly what they are. 'Army of the Deep' has a nice ring to it, don't you think? Or would do if the consequences weren't so dreadful."

Myfanwy was leaning her hand against the righted table to steady herself, pushing her fist into the wood. "Whose army?"

"Well, that's the question, isn't it? The creature walked in here tonight and asked for orders. Who, or what, is supposed to be giving them these orders?"

"He had an English accent," I blurted.

I regretted it instantly. It was normally me who was exasperated by Ludo's flouting of various secrecy rules. But tired and overwhelmed, I let my mouth escape me.

Both Myfanwy and Beryl glared hard at me. It was the first time I hadn't been pleased to see Beryl's face

Ludo's expression was more thoughtful.

"English?" Beryl asked slowly.

Myfanwy had added the sums quicker. "English?" she demanded. "Are you telling me that you English are behind all of this? That you're the bastards responsible?"

With a sigh, Ludo took another gulp of his whiskey. It may have seemed a casual gesture, but the amount of time he held that mug to his lips showed he was considering what might be the right words to use.

Finally, he lowered his drink and took a deep breath. "The tabloid press always has great fun reporting the esoteric and strange schemes the Nazis toyed with during the war. The more mystical the better. But even with a stiff upper lip and us tending to keep our feet more firmly on the ground, we had a whole secret department given over to similar types of research. Similar types of schemes. Years after the war, we were still actively investigating the existence of supernatural creatures which might provide us with an advantage.

"History is of course written by the victors, so we've managed to gloss over a lot of that stuff. But I'm going to guess that whatever is there in the bay, it's one of Britain's experiments gone horribly and belatedly awry."

"An experiment?" The rage had risen to the boil in Myfanwy. She jerked away from the table and took a stride towards Ludo, her hands spread preparatory to strangling him. There may have been something of the school mistress about Myfanwy, but Ludo was the true embodiment of the English public school. A boy who'd actually attended (for some reason I'd never got to the bottom of) both Shrewsbury and Eton. Absolutely, he was the most Establishment figure either of these women were ever likely to have met. The most English of Englishmen.

The words seethed like a loaded hiss from Myfanwy's pursed lips. "Are you telling me that this, all of this – all of the bloody misery we've had to endure – is a careless experiment created by *your lot*?"

"I can assure you, Myfanwy, this happened years before I was born."

"Your father then! Your uncle! Some other Englishman with an entitled manner who felt he had the right to destroy this town in a failed experiment!"

"Neither my father nor my uncles worked on this, Myfanwy. I assure you of that. And neither Garris nor I actually work for the British government. What is happening here is nothing to do with us."

"What is this experiment supposed to do?" asked Beryl

With Myfanwy stood menacingly over him, I think Ludo was happy for the distraction, a chance to fix his gaze elsewhere.

He blew out his cheeks. "I'm assuming a hell of a lot here, but I think it's pretty much working as it's supposed to," he told her. "The point of it would seem to be to drag the local men into the sea – hypnotise them, overwhelm their senses – and when they're drowned, reanimate them and turn them into soldiers for the Crown. Then, once us British had this 'Army of the Deep', to issue them with orders to march on Berlin, or wherever. So, apart from geographic location and not having those orders, I think it's probably working the way it should. The boffins behind it, if any of them are still alive, would no doubt be very happy with the results. It's just a shame that it sank here and got activated now, as opposed to off enemy territory in 1944."

An unwelcome tone of admiration had slipped into his voice. Fortunately he caught my eye and stopped himself, otherwise Myfanwy might have attempted to throttle him and the whole Army of the Deep couldn't have pulled her off.

Beryl continued to stroke her hands through Jason Jenkins' hair, the expression on her face one of utter sadness. "Are they going to come every night from now on?" she asked. "How do we stop this?"

Myfanwy snapped: "Mr Carstairs is going to call Whitehall, or whoever the hell is responsible, and get them to turn it off, aren't you?"

"Of course, I will," he nodded. "Of course.

However, I think we may need to do a bit more than that."

"More?" asked Beryl.

He raised the coffee mug to his lips and seemingly imbibed every molecule of whiskey. Once again my mug sat pretty much untasted by my side; my stomach turned at the smell of it.

"Tell me," he said softly. "Once our unfortunate guest had come in, once we'd handcuffed him to the wall, there was a heavy banging at the door. That wasn't an aural hallucination in our minds, was it? That was real. What happened?"

Myfanwy stared at Beryl. She still stood above Ludo, but her fist was pressing into the grain of the table again. Obviously, despite the strength she exuded, the memory of the night disturbed her.

Beryl actually answered. "They came in here. Three of them. The three youngest and strongest, I suppose. They were Dai Jones, Kevin Radcliffe and Richard Jenkins." She gasped, although managed to keep her voice level. "All of them I'd grown up with, all of them had been my friends. Now, they don't look like themselves anymore. I could recognise them, but they were all so different. It was like they'd done more than die. More than come back. They'd changed completely.

"We'd locked the basement door, as you told us, but we hadn't locked the front door of the house. We thought that once Jason finished talking to you, there'd be a signal and we'd let him out. That he'd be coming through the house again. We'd gone upstairs to the bedroom to look through the window, watching them mill about, waiting for a call from you. The men, or the things that used to be our men, weren't doing much in particular. They were loitering, lingering. It was like they were totally harmless.

"But then, I don't know how to describe it – for those three it seemed like energy suddenly shot into them. From nowhere, they discovered a purpose. They stopped what they were doing and charged straight to this house. Moving fast, much faster than I'd have imagined them being able to move. They barged through the front door and went straight to the basement, knowing exactly where they had to go. Then the three of them tried to smash the door down with their fists.

"It's as you said, Mr Carstairs, they're incredibly strong. They banged against the wood, so loud and vicious, we could hear the door rattling in the frame. We stayed hidden upstairs, not sure what to do." She stared away with undeserved embarrassment. "We were too scared to do anything at all. All we could hope was that the door would hold. Hoped you'd be okay. Because if they got through, who knows what they were going to do to you?"

Ludo nodded his appreciation for the telling. "And then they stopped?"

"Yes, a few minutes before dawn broke on the horizon, I guess, they turned and – as casual as you'd want – ambled away again. As if they had no purpose at all, as if they were lazy men who wanted to go and have a dip in the sea."

"Before daylight," Ludo mused. "They were obviously designed as a stealth army, to operate at night and scare the hell out of opposing forces. Although sunlight being actually fatal to them is clearly one hell of a design flaw."

"Maybe they dry out?" I suggested.

He nodded. "Or there's a power they draw from the

darkness that daylight mitigates. Still, one would have imagined they'd have thought that through before deploying the Mandrake. Strange. But in times of war, projects are often rushed into service before they're finished."

It wasn't pride in his tone this time, but more academic interest. As if it was a story he was hearing about rather than involved in. Again a red glare of fury rose to Myfanwy's cheeks. Ludo hastily bent his head in apology.

"Presumably," he said, "the body of Jason Jenkins, and those other men, must have passed by the women of Beddnic on the way here?"

"Of course," Myfanwy told him. "We took only the most sensible risks, but there was no avoiding some near brushes."

"And did it do anything to any of you? Reach for you? Treat you as a threat in anyway?"

"He's a he, not an it!" Beryl cried.

"I'm afraid it's an it now," Ludo's tone was as sympathetic as he could make it. "As much as I hate to state that fact, it's true, I'm sorry, but there's no getting around it."

"None of them came after us," Myfanwy said sombrely.

"After they saw you? Knew you were near? When they realised you'd led their designated speaker into a trap?"

"No."

He shot me a glance.

I knew exactly where he was going. "They don't hurt the women. 'The women are us'."

"Exactly! It's very chivalrous of them. The way a gentleman would choose to run a war." He stood up.

Perhaps a little slowly, maybe not as sprightly as when he was at his best, but with more energy than I could immediately muster. "Myfanwy, Beryl, if I could please ask you another favour? I want you to get every woman in this village onto the beach in an hour. I'm going to need to speak to you all."

15. A HORRIBLE THING TO ASK

Ludo and I stood in the cold breeze on the beach, with the women of Beddnic facing us.

Seen together, they were a motherhood of tiredness. Each had dark bags under their eyes, lines of worry cut into their foreheads, a grey pallor that spoke of weeks of anxiety. They all seemed to have dressed hastily, in blouses that weren't ironed, in skirts that were crumpled, in cardigans which weren't buttoned properly. It was as if the normal order of life had been suspended. They appeared weary, beaten, arms crossed in wariness as they pondered what dreadfulness might confront them next.

Staring at them, Ludo clearly needed to compose himself. He opened his mouth once and then closed it with no words emerging. Doubtless he was reconsidering the message he had to give, or at least how he was going to frame it.

"These men who come here each night are not your loved ones." He told them finally, his voice softer than normal, barely heard above the music of the waves.

"I'm sorry to have to tell you that, really I am. I know that where there's life there is normally hope, and to see those men stagger to your village and your homes each and every night gives the full impression of life. But no, I'm afraid the truth of it is that these men are not your loved ones. They are something else. They are tools of something else. And this *something else* is using your loved ones as puppets in the most cruel and unconscionable way.

"I can only imagine the hurt it causes you to see and hear your loved ones every evening. To watch them approach and hope that the deadness behind their eyes is negated by the fact that they're moving, that they're going to their local public house, that they're trying to go home. But I am afraid that they are actually gone. Gone forever. And I'm genuinely sorry to be the one who has to confirm that."

There were no sobs or gasps. No angry cries of disbelief. Each of the women was undeniably sad in their own uniquely crushed and broken way. The pain was universal, but you could see different degrees of it in their eyes. From a harsh acceptance that somehow life was always this way, to tears trickling freshly and without sobs down their cheeks. But none of them protested. Despite any hope they'd harboured, all of them knew deep in their hearts that Ludo was giving voice to an awful, and unavoidable, fact. Even Beryl, who stood at the edge of the group, in nothing more than blue jeans and black t-shirt – swaying a little in the breeze – could clearly see the truth in Ludo's words.

"What's caused this," he continued, "I don't exactly know. It's something uncanny and inexplicable. Undoubtedly there are people from long ago behind it – scientists who thought they were doing right, while really getting everything so, so wrong – but what they harnessed and how they thought they could control it, I have no idea. I'm sure they'd be mortified if they knew the calamity they'd unleashed on this beautiful little British village. This *Welsh* village. The whys and hows are an issue for another day. I will make sure it is all properly investigated, I promise you that. What's important right now though, is how we stop it. How we end all of this, so that you decent and wonderful women can try to have a restful night's sleep again.

"This morning, I will be making calls and giving instructions to get a team out there to the seabed. To put an end to whatever is causing this. Whatever it is that's luring men into the water. But I'm afraid that once the Mandrake is disabled, it won't actually halt the visitations from the deep each night.

"I'm sorry, I wish I could offer you reassurance that one would automatically equal the other, but I'd be lying to you if I did.

"Destroying HMS Mandrake and the signals it's giving out – the lure it's putting on every man who comes near – might stop the men it has already caught returning, but somehow I doubt it. My bet is, whatever is at work here, was designed to make do without the ship. For now it's a useful base, but eventually it was surely supposed to sail away and snare a whole other group of men. It couldn't have floated there for long without attracting the attention of the Luftwaffe, so it would have moved on and left its Army of the Deep behind. If I'm right about that, no matter if we blow the ship to ten thousand rusty pieces, *they* will keep coming. The remains of your men will continue walking this beach until they are nothing but rotting husks.

"We have to stop them. We have to make sure that tonight is the last of their nocturnal visits and – I'm sorry – but as far as I can see, there's only one way we can do that."

He trailed off. Staring at the small crowd of old, young, slim, rounded, tall, short women in front of him – each of them desperate and fraught – he evidently wished there was something else, anything else, he could ask of them.

After a long pause, he finally – although imperceptibly to anyone who hadn't worked at his side for the last few months – steeled himself. He swallowed, straightened his shoulders and stared at the green Welsh hills beyond. Best to try and get through the rest of what he had to say without his gaze settling upon a sad pair of eyes.

"There's only one thing we can do," he repeated, "and it's not going to be easy.

"I'm sorry about this, I really am. If there was any alternative I could think of, then I would instantly make that Plan A. But there isn't. There's only this and it's a huge ask, but it's all I can think of to bring this to a close.

"These creatures, these things that used to be your men, they can't hurt you. They told us so themselves. And they have demonstrated that fact night after night. I don't know why this should be the case, whether they're conditioned in some gentlemanly way to never hurt any woman, or whether they recognise you as British women – the ones they are supposedly fighting for – and that means they cannot harm you. Whatever the reason, no matter what happens, they are not going to hurt any of the women of this village.

"That's one thing we know. We have also learned

that like the vampire of stories, sunlight is fatal to them. Although 'fatal' may not be the most appropriate word. So, if before dawn, we can stop them getting into the water, this will be over. All of this will end. We will have the dead returned to us and we can treat their bodies in a decent way, as opposed to the monstrousness whatever out there has been dealing in.

"You will have your village again, no longer will you have to cower in fear. It will never be the same, that is obvious, but the remains of your men will be cared for properly. They will sleep the decent sleep of the hereafter."

Staring at the horizon, he hesitated at what was coming next. Already knowing what his plan was, I tightened my fists in anticipation. Picking up on my nervousness – or maybe needing my support – Beryl's eyes met mine. They were sad and frightened, but I could sense – that no matter what he was going to ask – she trusted the two of us to do the right thing.

"Tonight," Ludo's voice rose in volume, "when they raise themselves from the water, tonight when they enter the town, I want you women – all of you – to stand together in a line right at the mouth of the cove. From one side to the other, blocking the way to the sea for those things that used to be your men."

There were no terrified gasps, no outraged cries – but in the silence, it was hard to miss the horror and revulsion at his words.

Ludo spoke faster. "You will stand there and link arms. Each and every one of you. I'm afraid it has to be that way, as otherwise the line won't stretch right across the cove. You will stand and lock arms and wait as a defiant line. Together, you will stop those things returning to the sea. As one, you will hold the line until sunrise, when all movement should die afresh in their limbs and then this will be over.

"I'm sorry to ask this of you. I really am so, so sorry, but there's nothing else I can think of. If we're going to end this, then we need you fine ladies of Beddnic to act as an unstoppable barrier."

Now there were murmurs, now there were sobs. One particular low groan of anguish emanated from an old lady in a floral housecoat.

Ludo knew he couldn't engage with their disbelief, he couldn't open this for debate – he had to press on, make sure he got all of the plan out.

"They won't harm you! They *can't* harm you. If you're in their way, they are not going to push you or shove you or knock you from your spot. No, they won't touch you, and so if you're standing in front of them – in front of them as a solid and unbreakable line between them and the sea – there will be nothing they can do about it. They will be trapped with no way to the water. Trapped with no way to return to whatever is down there to nourish and support them. Trapped, so that when sunrise comes they will collapse, they will be beaten. Whatever motivation keeps them going, whatever source they draw their energy from, that will come to an end and this – all of this – will be finished for good.

"I'm not going to lie, this is going to be so horrifically difficult for every one of you. All the faces before you will be ones you recognise. You will see your loved ones come down the beach towards you, desperate to get past you. Maybe the muscularity of their faces will be such that they can look at you imploringly. Try to meet your eyes and reassure you with a familiar glance that, really – hidden inside – they remain your loved ones. But that's not the case. That will be a cruel deception.

"Deep in your hearts, you already know this. In the last few weeks you have seen the bodies of your loved ones moving around like movie zombies. You have seen it every night and that vision has not brought you succour or relief. Instead, it has hurt you to the core. And this is your chance to put it to an end.

"It will be incredibly hard. These are the bodies of your fathers, your sons, your brothers, your lovers, your friends. And at dawn tomorrow – if you do this right, if you hold a solid line – they will seem to die right in front of you. They will go from movement and a dull light in the eyes, to nothing. I'm so sorry, ladies, I wish it could be another way. But if you can do this, it will be over. It will be done. The bodies of your men may seem to die in front of you all over again, but they are dead already and their remains will at least be home. You will have closure. You can bury them, cremate them, treat them in a dignified fashion. This horrible period will be brought to a close and you will be able to start – as impossible as it seems – to put together the pieces of your lives. I promise you that. This hardness will be worth it, I absolutely promise you."

The tears and wails were an infection which had taken over this sadness of women. By now, all of them were crying; shaking their heads as they thought of the horror they had already endured and the fresh horror they must face.

Myfanwy, when she spoke, seemed to have shrunk to such an extent that she was like a frightened little girl. "It's cruel what you're asking us to do, Mr Carstairs, so utterly cruel."

"I know," he told her regretfully. "Believe me, I

know."

16. DOING THE MEN'S WORK FOR THEM

As we walked from the beach, Beryl clutched hold of my hand. Squeezing it tight, perhaps in the hope that it could give her the resolve and strength she needed. For a while as we walked, slowly side by side, hand in hand, neither of us said anything. A silence that seemed to match the quiet of the surroundings, the brittleness of the atmosphere.

"I'm sorry," I whispered, finally.

It was possibly a whole minute before she replied. "It's not your fault, Mr Garris. You can't imagine that I think this is your fault at all."

"But I feel bad anyway. We came here to help you," I said, staring at the narrow entrance to the cove, "and this doesn't feel close to helping anymore."

At the top of the beach, both Ludo and an ashen Myfanwy were circulating amongst the women. Trying to reassure them that this was the right course of action, that – despite how awful it sounded – they could manage it.

Beryl stifled a sob. "You came here to do the best you could and I believe you have, haven't you?"

"I've tried. Both of us have tried. But, I'm thinking of your father and your friends and everyone else here who was loved, and wondering if it's enough."

She shook her head. "Dad always said he could look after himself. That's what he told us when he moved out. I was young then, but I remember it so clearly. He said that he could look after himself, so he didn't need Mam to be constantly fussing over him. It would be better if he had his space, he said, and she could spend more time fussing over me. But he couldn't look after himself at all." There was a slight smile on her face, enough in the memory to cheer her as well as hurt her. "He got a room above the pub, but kept coming home for dinner. He even tried to take his washing to Mam, until she put him straight on that. He said he wanted to move because he wanted to look after himself, make his own way in the world, but he got no more than a street away. Nowhere further than that."

She sighed and any hint of a smile slipped from her face. "Mam always had to help Dad. As I grew up, I always had to help him too – like he was the child. This then feels just another thing I've got to do for him. The stupid bastard couldn't even die properly, he needs a helping hand in that as well. That's what we've got to do tonight. Help our men do a job that they should have been capable of doing properly themselves."

Again she went for a smile, but it didn't stick this time and instead she dissolved into sobs. Her hand stayed in mine and she kept walking. Shaking her head to try and remove the tears from her cheeks.

We fell into another silence. One that was too full of emotion to be truly companionable. As we reached the pub, the true heart of the town – there to feed and water the weary fishermen – she turned and stared at the sea. Back to the rest of the women and the grey thrashing waves beyond.

Beryl squeezed my fingers so tight.

"Have you ever lost anyone, Mr Garris?" she asked, keeping her voice admirably level.

"Not really," I confessed. "My parents are both alive, as are my brother and sister. I suppose though, that I'm in the slightly odd position of having lost more than one colleague."

"Colleagues?" Her eyebrow raised, before settling without murmur into a smooth, concentrated, impassiveness. Clearly this was the only way she was going to get through. To give in to the tumult of emotions she faced would most likely be to crumble.

"Mine isn't a particularly normal job."

"Was it horrible?"

"I was there when one of them passed. Close enough I should have been able to do something. And yes, it was utterly horrible."

There was perhaps the unspoken question of whether it was as horrible as what now faced her. But the answer to that was no. Not close.

Beryl watched Ludo on the beach, being as solicitous as I had ever seen him. "What about Mr Carstairs?" she asked. "He talks big, but he has sad eyes."

"He's lost people too."

"Who?" she asked, but then raised her fingers to stall me. "I'm sorry, Mr Garris. *That* really and obviously isn't any of my business."

I squeezed her hand to reassure her. "Michael," I murmured.

"I'm sorry?"

"Please call me Michael. I'd prefer it."

She smiled at me. A flash of a real grin tantalisingly on her lips. Despite the lines on her forehead and the darkness under her eyes, she had such an incredibly gorgeous smile. It was there, waiting for happier times to come to her.

"Michael," she repeated. "I think the name Michael is cool."

"I'm glad, Beryl." I tried a smile, but failed to match hers. "I'll be honest, you're the first Beryl I've ever met. And I don't think I've heard a prettier name."

She blushed and turned her head away, then the wind blew past us and we both fixed our gazes on the mouth of the cove and the sea beyond.

"Everything comes to an end," she intoned at last. "I had such a happy childhood here. Even with Dad frequently being a bit of a prick, I had such a good childhood. Obviously I knew I was going to leave one day. I've always wanted to go to San Francisco. See how their bay compares to ours." She gave a mirthless laugh that was immediately lost on the breeze. "I always thought I'd come home again. I know that everything comes to an end, but I always thought that there'd be a welcome for me here. You know, this would always be the place I called home." She sighed, "I guess some endings are more brutal than others."

17. THE ONLY MEN ANYWHERE NEAR BEDDNIC

Ludo and I – still the only men anywhere near Beddnic – made our way up the steep hill behind the village.

December was cruel. There wasn't enough daylight for us to allay every fear, for us to think through every contingency. The night would be long.

He'd made it clear that he wanted us to be outside too, for us to see what happened this night. He didn't want to shut himself away in the basement again. We owed the women of Beddnic that, he said, we had to be with them in some manner.

I agreed entirely.

The beach was obviously too close. In fact we couldn't hope to be safe and immune anywhere in Beddnic itself. So we found a spot on the hill behind that offered a good overview. Both of us wrapped in thick coats and scarves – mine borrowed from Beryl, and Ludo's from Myfanwy – we trekked to a small copse halfway up. The cove itself was too wind battered for much to grow there, but there was a small grouping of sycamore trees that had somehow proven themselves against the elements.

With the sun setting at our backs, and the biting cold already chapping our lips and cracking the skin of our knuckles, we pulled the rusty chain twice around the biggest and strongest tree and once again slammed the cold metal of the manacles around our wrists. We sat there hoping that we'd avoid the worst of the effects. Ludo wanted to see it, he kept saying, to actually witness what happened. He wanted to make sure it was all over.

The Chief had done his utmost, but the sea had been too choppy for divers to get down there today. It was impossible for them to find and then attach depth charges to the rusting hulk of the Mandrake. And since we hadn't determined precisely where it was as yet, there was no way we could drop bombs from high on the off-chance. Tomorrow the weather looked fairer. He promised Ludo that with the sea calmer, he would throw every resource he could muster at it.

So it was one more night and the two of us were doing all we could to minimise the effects of the Mandrake's call, while still being present.

"Given this whole cove is basically a large echo chamber," Ludo observed ruefully. "It may be a fool's ambition to imagine we can stay here and in any way keep our wits about us."

Before we came up, we'd watched the undoubtedly terrified women of Beddnic form a line across the front of the cove. A practise run. The cold December sea lapped at their ankles and the only piece of tiny reassurance they had was that the tide was going out. All of them together, they about stretched the full length of it. They managed to get from one side to the other and do what Ludo needed them to do. It was tight though. Maybe if one woman fell from the line, the remaining arms could stretch and fill the gap. But if two women dropped away, then there would be a space, a way through and their efforts would be futile.

Ludo thanked them for their efforts, praised them for their steadfastness. It might have been the tiredness getting the better of him, but I had never seen his blue eyes so full of emotion.

I had faith in these women. Despite everything, I was confident in their resolve. Whatever lay ahead may be horrible, but I knew that between them they had the courage to see this through. To end it once and for all.

As Ludo and I sat there on the hill, we knew there was nothing extra we could do. Whatever was going to happen was going to happen now.

With a sigh I asked. "What do you think will become of this place after all this?"

The sun was setting and Ludo stared to the horizon. He squinted, deep lines etched into his forehead. His sandy and matted hair had been without a brush for days.

"It's difficult to say, isn't it, Garris? You'd hope the village would survive, as it's such a pretty spot and it would be a shame for it to become an abandoned ruin full of ghosts and ghoulish memories. All the history contained here – the generations of families who have called this village home – undoubtedly it would be a terrible shame. But equally, I ask myself, can it really survive? Can it actually get through this? The women who live here have been through so much, are they actually going to stay with all the reminders of it each and every day? And if they choose to, how will they bring in more men to keep Beddnic going? More people? Who is going to come here when it has such a stink of death? But then, maybe I don't know what I'm talking about. It's more than possible that having run away all of my life, I'm not qualified to talk about people whose dream it is to calmly settle down. To lay roots and know that the place of their beloved childhood will be there at the end of their lives. Maybe, for some of these people – some of these wonderfully resolute ladies – the sense of home is so high that nothing will ever drive them away from here. Nothing at all."

The beach was quiet. There was ten minutes to sunset and that line wouldn't need to be formed for hours, not until they could be as sure as they could be that every one of the creatures who used to be their men was out of the sea.

When we stared at the beach, it was hard not to imagine them there. A hopefully indomitable barrier.

"What do *you* think?" he asked.

"I hope the village survives. I want to do all I can to make sure it survives, to help with the future."

Ludo nodded once. "You don't necessarily have to stay here, you know? I'm sure if you ask her she'll come with you."

Neither of us said anything more for a while. We instead watched the dusk fall and the beach sink into a purplish darkness, lit only by the full moon. Waiting for the first moment when the waves broke rudely apart and one of the creatures started to make its way towards land.

"Do you think this will work?" I asked in a whisper.

As we inserted our earplugs, he answered, "If anyone can make it work, it's these women."

18. THE FINAL NIGHT

As always, it came upon us incredibly quickly.

I can remember watching the moon reach a decent height in the sky, and then my mind melted away.

The girth of the tree trunk between us stopped Ludo reaching for my wrist this time. I think he did stretch out, but I was too far away.

Without his sharp nails digging under the white bandages and attacking my skin again, I had nothing to hold onto. His voice was a distant, unintelligible echo. There was no way I could focus on it, it was an irritating background sound that was so easy to ignore.

The way the moon kissed the undulating waves was gorgeous. They lapped in and out, in and out, shining brightly. It wasn't the grey old sea anymore, it was more something from a fairy tale.

The roar of the tide overwhelmed me.

Surely it didn't actually roar, the tide was retreating and it was a calm night. But my perception was such that the sound buzzed through my ears and overwhelmed my thoughts. It blotted every other sensation from my head.

Gasping, I strained at my metal bond. It was like I could feel the water. The moon was high in the sky and the clouds were gone and yet, it was raining on me. I could actually sense the rainwater touching my skin. Cool, glorious, glimmering moisture running over my face and calling me towards the beautiful sea below.

Even then, a faint voice – almost lost at the farthest edge of my mind – assured me that it couldn't be real rain. It was unlike any rain I'd ever felt. The water seemed to hammer into me, but didn't sting or irritate. I didn't suffer cold or even damp that night. Instead I felt I was showering under a hot, natural fountain. A sensation soothing and full of relief, making me feel the way I was always supposed to feel. In that water, I was me at my best.

"Garris!" I heard Ludo yell. "Try to stay with me, Garris. I know it's hard, but you have to focus!"

Maybe I did stare over in his direction. A small blob of a man in a dark duffel coat. He was nothing to me right then though. I barely recognised him. He didn't gleam or shine. It was obvious, just by looking at him, that he wouldn't be both cool and warm to the touch. There was no magic to his solid mass. He wasn't the water and the only thing that mattered right then was the water.

I turned my head – every muscle in my face and body straining – and yelled towards the sea. Letting it know I was there, that I was ready for it. My vocal chords seemed to rip open. The sound trying to rival the roar of the waves and the pelting of the rain. Desperately I cried out, not wanting to be ignored and forgotten. Tonight they had to take me with them. I wanted, with all my being, to be part of what they were.

When they came out of the water, staggering and stumbling as always, the creatures who used to be the men of Beddnic were recognisably my friends.

They were obviously my brothers.

The Army of the Deep was calling to me, wanting me to join them.

And I so wanted to enlist.

As always, they ambled up the beach. Soldiers in a war they didn't understand, warriors who hadn't been given any clear orders and so fell onto a base instruction to observe. Reconnaissance, the creature who had once been Jason Jenkins had called it. And that's exactly what it was. This one isolated village, this cut-off community, and because they had nowhere else to be and no other instruction, they came at night observing. Remembering who they used to be, with no fresh directions to override that.

Maybe if they'd seen Ludo and I – or a Ludo and I who'd retained hold of our faculties – they wouldn't have been the shambling, unhurried group they were. We'd already proven ourselves dangerous, after all.

But right then, I didn't think of that. There was no concept of plans or strategies. Nothing so calculated could break through the fuzz in my mind. All I wanted to do was be with them and *be* them.

To join the ranks of these ambling men who glimmered exquisitely as they watched and observed – and who didn't notice the wall of raincoat clad women close shut behind them.

My memory of that night – in fact, my memory of all those nights – is a series of discordant sounds, images and feelings. I can't accurately state in what order any of it transpired. It's all a blur, like I was staring at the world from the bottom of a murky pool.

A pool that didn't glow refreshingly, but was instead filled with dirt and blood.

Yet one thing I do remember clearly is that line of women closing off the route from Beddnic to the sea.

The women themselves seemed to possess a visible energy.

Now I think of it as a warm glow, a red fuzzy outline to each body which burned bright and quietly powerful. But on the hillside – staring at the beach while the men staggered around the village – I could only see the danger of it. I could recognise it in a way none of my brethren from the deep seemingly could.

There's an image in my mind of Ludo scrabbling around the tree, then grabbing to me through the shadows. Somehow keeping himself together while I fell apart. He was trying to help me, to keep me calm.

Desperately I tried to cling on to who I was. But with every crash of the waves, the allure of the sea grew stronger. I didn't want to be stranded on that fucking hill, I needed to be in the water where it was *safe*.

I wanted to join them all. To be at the heart of the brotherhood. It shames me to admit it, but all I could think of was helping them.

And so I screamed. Yelled to my brothers about the women. Those women glowed red and I knew already that we couldn't touch that which glowed red. They were to be protected. However, they were blocking off our route to the sanctuary of the water.

Surely there had to be another way around. If I could alert the men soon enough, we would all have time to find it. If my brothers in the village realised what was happening, they could carve another route to the place that was safe, the sea. The sea!

The sky was a bright clear moonlit night, yet it felt

like I was on the hill in the pouring rain. Luscious, beautiful water dripping off me. Flowing into my nose and mouth and claiming me. That chain pulled me against the tree, tighter it seemed as I struggled with everything I had against it. Frantically, I attempted to squeeze my fingers through the manacle to break myself free.

"Garris!" I heard Ludo yell, so loudly and frequently as to make himself hoarse. "Garris! Please focus!"

I don't know how long I screamed, or for how long Ludo yelled his entreaties at me.

The women stood there resilient. Their line unyielding.

December nights are long, but it seemed we didn't have enough time.

In my heightened state, I could feel dawn coming long before it arrived. It was like a sickness. My skin grew clammy, an echoing thump rose from the depths of my mind. Redness was coming to the sky and redness was our enemy. This low winter sun, to my eyes, was a burning cauldron.

I felt it burn into every inch of me, then watched as – horribly – a panic started to rise through my brothers.

Helpless on the hillside, I stood and witnessed the realisation come over those poor men: they were trapped.

That glowing line of red on the beach appeared unbreakable. The women were not moving. Their arms were interlocked, their spirit awe-inspiring.

However, that's not how it felt to me right then.

I screamed with abject terror.

Slowly, unable to move with great speed even at a time of such peril, the Army of the Deep stumbled its way down from the village, onto the beach. Then they stood and stared with blank expressions at the burning line in front of them. The line they couldn't cross. It was quiet, they never lost their stillness, but desperately their eyes hunted for another way. Their tired minds trying to fathom a new route to take them to the blessed water.

If only I could have communicated with them earlier. We would have had time to find another way.

These were British women formed in a line to obstruct them, and there was no way we could harm British women. It simply couldn't be done.

So, with each man turning in lost circles on the beach, they stared around that closed bay mouth and hunted in vain for escape. Their minds were decayed by seawater and barely flickering, yet the impulse was impossible to ignore. Every sinew of their beings strained for the sea. But this was an army designed to do nothing except follow orders and no orders had been forthcoming. Without them, there was no way they could work out a route to salvation. The sky would be genuinely red soon and they couldn't be on land when the sky was red. They knew that; however there was nothing they could do.

Some headed towards the rocks, doubtless intent on finding a path to carry them through. Scale the side of the cliffs perhaps, go over the women – not that they had the balance or motor abilities to seriously do that. First one and then another fell – their hands still grappling thin air – onto the jagged pebbles. They landed broken on the rough ground and their brethren trampled over them. This was not an army which needed every member to come back. No, it was the ultimate disposable fighting force. Not thinking at all of the broken bones and ruptured flesh beneath them, these creatures that used to be men employed the bodies as a writhing bridge to try and get themselves through.

There was no path however. No chance of them scaling the sheer walls of the cliffs.

Those women held together even as others of the army stood in front of them; like they were trying to beg the women to relent, to part, to let them through. Possibly hoping that a body and a face which had once belonged to a loved one would soften, rather than harden, their hearts.

It must have been horrible for the women to see the decomposing bodies of the men they'd loved, but the line stayed firm. It held.

I didn't realise it at the time, I couldn't see it from my vantage point, but more than half the women were facing out to the sea. They were staring away from whatever horror was behind them. I'm sure even then a good few clamped their eyes shut.

Only a couple had the stomach to stand there and watch what was happening.

Myfanwy and Beryl amongst them.

As the sun started to lighten the sky (to my eyes it was like the reverberations of a dreadful nuclear explosion), the army – these beautiful brothers of mine – stood rigid and started to sway on their feet. The strength in their limbs vanished, the momentum they needed to press forward wore down.

There was a final gasp of defiance. Sickening roars into the sky, aimed at the sun and the fate they could do nothing about. Then one by one, the poor creatures collapsed onto the pebbles of the beach.

A large percentage of the women may have had their backs turned and their eyes closed, but there weren't anywhere near enough earplugs to go around. They must have heard dull thud after dull thud, as decaying flesh and bone smacked onto the watery beach. It was what remained of their loved ones, but knowing they were finally coming to a proper rest wouldn't have made the experience of that sound – and that sound repeated again and again – any more pleasant.

Still chained to the tree, I could nonetheless experience the strength seeping from those men. Every time one of my brethren fell, something inside me was twisted around.

There was a kind of life within them. It wasn't human, but instead something inconceivable to me – older and stranger and yet so, so wonderful. I could feel it as a new, extraordinary form of being. Even as the sunlight streamed over the horizon, it felt part of me and I was part of it.

But now its emissaries were being killed. That force within them cruelly extinguished on this cold, dark, Welsh beach.

How close to real dawn we were, I don't know. My eyes saw a blooming pink sky, a colour which had to be feared.

I was screaming. I felt I spent every second of that night roaring desperately. With any molecule of strength I could muster in my body, I was wrestling against the manacle. My only purpose was to be free, to help those wonderful men below.

The manacles themselves may have been new, but the chain was old and had spent each of the last three nights being strained against mightily.

Some time before full dawn, it happened.

As I yanked against it, as I pulled my whole weight

down the hillside and gave everything I had, one of the interlocking chains snapped and the whole thing broke apart.

Such was the force I'd employed, I tumbled helplessly as it gave way. Not falling with a thud to the ground in front of me, but rolling halfway down the hill towards Beddnic. My body crashing onto stones and my skin tearing open over brambles. A big, relieved smile on my face the whole time.

"Garris!" Ludo's voice seemed from another universe. "For god's sake, Garris!"

I'd fallen too far for him to reach out and grab me. He told me later that with the chain loose from around the tree, he knew he couldn't come any closer anyway. Despite the sun rising, the pulse of the deep would have dominated his mind too.

There's not much I can recall from my bruising downhill journey. Once I'd pulled myself from the jagged rock on which I'd crashed to a halt, I ran on trembling legs – loose and uncoordinated. Keeping my balance simply by luck, or maybe because that force from beyond was tugging me inexorably. I have in my mind flashes of Beddnic village itself – the pub and the shop and all the deserted houses – as I shakily made my way onto the beach.

In the sky, the hellish red sun was burning off the morning mist. I could barely glance at the orb, the glare hurt my eyes too much. My heart pounded as I rushed forward – desperate to save my brethren and craving the cool sanctuary of the water.

I could see the Army of the Deep dying once again, even as they were already rotting. And I thought if I could get through the red line myself, I could find safety in the sea. If I could force my way through, maybe one or two of my brothers could follow me and save themselves as well.

So I charged forward, my limbs aching with exertion. The women glowed at the edge of the bay – a shining, impenetrable barrier. My brothers couldn't touch them, but maybe I could. There had to be a door through, I just had to find a way to prise it open myself.

As I raced down the beach, I think I cried from the bottom of my lungs: a mad yell of fury, hurt and frustration.

That line of women was in front of me, a barrier to all that was good. I was running towards it, knowing I couldn't smash it apart, but hoping if I was forceful enough it would split in the face of me and my anger. None of my brethren were as strong as me under the sunlight, that's why it was up to me to save them.

And as I got near – the smell of the sea so close it tingled my nostrils – the line broke a little. A small part of it separated from the rest and lurched towards to me.

Two soft hands grabbed me. Beautiful arms clutching me tight and forcing me backwards.

I had no strength left in my limbs. The tumble from the hill had taken too much from me and, despite the crash of the sea filling my mind, I dropped feebly onto the pebbles.

The intensity of the noise lessened and the desperation which had driven me faded. It became an echo. In a few seconds, it was barely there at all. My ears filled with the gentle lapping of the waves. One of many different noises of the seaside.

The sun was a faint orb. Only a few shades brighter than white – the way it should be, the way it really was. I panted as I stared up at it, great gasps of air which shuddered right through my being.

The arms which had grabbed me squeezed me tight. A whispered voice telling me: "It's all going to be okay, Michael. It's finally going to be okay."

And that's how I started that morning – the first hopeful day in Beddnic for far too long – lying cold, wet, tired and confused on the beach. With Beryl holding me and stroking her fingers through my hair, assuring me that everything was finally going to be fine.

19. THE BEACH OF DEATH

For the first time in weeks, the road was opened and men were allowed to drive into the village.

Every task which needed to be done was performed with great sensitivity. Counsellors had been put on standby and arrived by the carload – three to a backseat – to provide the women with as much care as they needed.

Beddnic beach was littered with bodies. There were screams and pained tears as the women had to walk back up, through the remains of their loved ones, into the village itself. Some of them refused to open their eyes and had to be led by hand to stop them brushing against something which used to be a man. As afternoon arrived, those bodies were removed as delicately as possible. I don't know how our organisation paid for it all, but each body was assigned his own personal undertaker. There was a man in a black coat dedicated to giving every individual the required tenderness and dignity.

Or as much tenderness and dignity which could be

offered while the whole matter was under heavy investigation and detailed autopsies needed to be carried out.

Of course, The Chief was one of the first to arrive. His black pinstripe Saville Row suit, which was pristine enough to pass muster on a parade ground, making myself and Ludo – bedraggled and wearing the same clothes three days straight – resemble an unfortunate sub-species.

I was sat at the breaker wall of the beach. From somewhere, Beryl had found me a thick tartan blanket, which she wrapped tenderly around my shoulders. Still I shivered. The cold felt like it was in my bones and was never going to go away.

Ludo was still sporting the coat from last night, the buttons open. Despite his tiredness, there was a buzz around him. It's what made him such a perfect agent, he was all ready for more.

The last of the hearses made its way towards the specially designated morgue, and the beach – to the unaware – now resembled any other part of the South Wales coast. To those who'd lived through it though, I can't imagine that it would ever seem the same again.

Nearly lying on the cold brick, I stared at the only two non-Organisation personnel who had chosen to venture onto the beach.

Myfanwy and Beryl had walked to the mouth of the cove, standing a few feet from the incoming tide. They had their arms around each other and were staring to the sea. Neither of them was uttering a word, but they were taking comfort from being together. Trained investigator that I am, it embarrassed me that I hadn't noticed it before – they were very clearly mother and daughter.

"I'm well aware this has a very tight time limit," The Chief was telling Ludo, "but our divers are down there now and once they've obtained all the extra information we can get for our investigations, they will lay charges and blow the whole thing to a million pieces. Don't worry, Carstairs, it will be completed before nightfall."

Ludo didn't so much as glance at his watch. "They've got about forty-five minutes, sir. If things haven't gone boom by then, this whole thing is going to start over."

"Why couldn't they just blow it this morning?" There was no way to hide the intense weariness of my voice.

The Chief had been sympathetic when he arrived, but his tone now was as if talking to a simpleton. "You know damn well that's not the way things work for us, Garris. We need to understand what's going on. It's practically our reason for existing."

I looked at the two women on the beach. Maybe Ludo followed my gaze, although knowing him he was probably already well aware they were there.

"What about the village?" he asked.

"We'll do all we can for these women. They can all have therapists for the next year if they want, I'll sign off on it. We'll do what we have to do and then we'll get out of their hair. Let the grieving process, the healing process, begin."

"So, no quarantine?"

The Chief shook his head. "I don't see the point in any quarantine. There's nothing in the town itself that's dangerous and the women are the survivors rather than the culprits. We'll move on our way. Let the place return to normal."

"As if that's remotely possible," I muttered.

I don't think either of them heard me.

"You two have done a damn good job here," The Chief continued. "I'm proud of both your efforts. I appreciate that you've been through something very close to hell, and frankly the two of you both look hellish and smell hellish. But I want to say, on the record, that I am immensely grateful that you got to the root of this problem with no further loss of life.

"Which makes it all the more awkward that I can't offer either of you any leave or recuperation time. I can't let you have more than a couple of hours to catch up with sleep, as clearly you both need sleep. The fact is that we have to understand what on earth has been going on here. The investigation always takes precedent over everything else, you know that. So, I require you both in London, with your reports filed and follow-ups undertaken. Apologies, but we have a grade seven incident happening in Lima as well, so we're stretched and I need you fellows doing all you can on this case."

A cold breeze blew past as a short silence pressed down on us. Neither Ludo nor I immediately responded. In the distance, I could hear a gull. A faint noise, but an unmistakable sign that normality was returning.

"I'll come with you," Ludo told him. "I'll come this second, if you want. But maybe give Garris here a day or two. Make sure that one of us is a bit fresher for the investigation. That way he'll be ready to grab hold of the slack when I eventually crash."

"Fair enough!" The Chief nodded once and shone his big bright grin in my direction. "You've got forty-eight hours' respite, Garris!"

I lay back on that damp wall, staring at Beryl and her mother swaying in the breeze in the distance, silently thanking Ludo Carstairs – my colleague and friend.

A Note from the author

If you enjoyed Call of the Mandrake, then do check out the other entries in The Ghostly Shadows series. The other terrifying instalments: Death at the Seaside, Certain Danger and Won't You Come Save Me are now available. Each is ostensibly a standalone, but if you read them all you'll start to recognise the connections…

In addition, if you have read and enjoyed this novella, would you please take the time to leave a short review of it on Amazon?

Reviews are the lifeblood of an indie author. They make the difference between scrabbling along and actually making a living out of our writing. So, if you're able to find the time to leave your thoughts on Call of the Mandrake – or any of my other Ghostly Shadows tales, long or short – then I would be tremendously grateful.

Kind regards,

FRJ.

OTHER BOOKS IN THE GHOSTLY SHADOWS SERIES

All available in paperback.

DEATH AT THE SEASIDE

Nothing was going to ruin Castle's holiday, except the mocking laughter of the dead…

Larry Castle was anticipating a lovely few days at the seaside. Basking in the sunshine, canoodling with his mistress and playing the big man visiting town. However, a chance encounter leaves his confidence reeling.

There's a possibility that someone knows his darkest secret. The thing that made him, but which could equally break him. No matter what, Castle is going to have to deal with this problem. Otherwise it could cost him everything.

This weekend Castle is going to confront the ghosts of his past, but some ghosts are more real than others…

Death at the Seaside – a gripping new supernatural thriller which could chill on even the most uncomfortably hot day.

The first in the Ghostly Shadows series.

CERTAIN DANGER

What are those voices from the past? And why are they screaming at her?

It all started when she witnessed a car crash. A brutal smash which left a gorgeous young couple dead. But for Alice, it reawakened strange memories of childhood: a sinister old house, a dead boy in the woods and an other-worldly power lurking forever in the darkness.

Desperate to make sense of the bizarre pictures in her mind, Alice's enquires lead her to a hidden away clinic in the Surrey Hills. Within those walls though, are the terrifying secrets she's been running from her whole life.

Now, for Alice, the truth could not only break apart her sanity, it could destroy the whole world…

Certain Danger – A brand new British horror tale perfect for all fans of James Herbert, Clive Barker, Iain Rob Wright and Hammer/Amicus films of the 1970s.

The second in the Ghostly Shadows series.

Won't You Come Save Me

The actress might be dead, but her voice keeps singing to him…

Something about that murdered woman got to the detective. She was a missing person he was tracing – a young starlet – but by the time he found her, she was a bloated corpse on a dockside. One moonless night she'd been beaten, strangled and dumped in the Thames.

Her gangster boyfriend thinks he's got away with murder, but the detective is coming for him. The need for revenge burning at his soul. He might look like an average man, but there's a new force within him – one that craves bloody vengeance…

Every night her song gets louder in his ears, but what will happen when its power is truly unleashed?

Won't You Come Save Me – A brand new British horror tale perfect for all fans of James Herbert, Clive Barker, Iain Rob Wright and Dennis Wheatley.

The third in the Ghostly Shadows series.

ALSO BY F.R. JAMESON
THE SCREEN SIREN NOIR SERIES

All available in paperback.

DIANA CHRISTMAS

He's been threatened, beaten and broken – but still he doesn't regret meeting the actress who disappeared…

Michael, a young film journalist, is sent to interview the reclusive movie star Diana Christmas. Twenty years prior, the red-headed starlet suddenly abandoned her career, leaving her fans puzzled and shocked.

Their attraction is instant. Between the sheets, Diana tells him of the blackmail and betrayal which ruined her. And how – even now – she's being tormented.

Emboldened, Michael sets out on a mission to track down a compromising roll of film – unaware that around the next corner lurks deadly peril.

Can Michael save Diana from her past? Or will the secrets which crushed her life destroy them both?

Diana Christmas: Blackmail, Death and a British Film Star – a new thriller of desire and betrayal from F.R. Jameson.

The first in the Screen Siren Noir series.

EDEN ST. MICHEL

Avenging her secret could put a noose around both their necks…

Joe might be a stuntman, but still he'd never expect to end up in bed with a genuine movie star. However, that's what happens the night he meets the ultra-glamorous, Eden St. Michel. Swiftly they're the talk of the town. Their passion fast, intense and dangerous.

But Eden has scars from her past, both mental and physical. Joe needs to be her hero, although retribution won't be easy. One misstep could mean the end of their careers and – maybe – their lives.

After a sudden moment of violence, Joe finds himself in deadly trouble. He may have the love of a good woman, yet it's leading him to the gallows.

But what if the only way to save Eden is to make that ultimate sacrifice?

Eden St. Michel: Scandal, Death and a British Film Star – a new tale of film stars, gangsters and death from F.R. Jameson.

The second book in the 'Screen Siren Noir' series.

ALICE RACKHAM

Theirs is an affair destined to end in murder!

Thomas had never met a woman like Alice Rackham. A film-star: sophisticated and uninhibited. Not only is their passion intense, but she could help this impoverished young actor with his own career. Surely it doesn't really matter that she has danger written all over her…

As he isn't the only one smitten with Alice: her ex-lover skulks ceaselessly outside her home and keeps a former policeman on retainer. A giant of a man who would relish making both their lives torture.

With Thomas rattled, Alice suggests a relaxing trip to an English country house. But trouble isn't just going to follow them out there, it's about to turn deadly.

Can Thomas save Alice from her past? Or will it destroy them both?

Alice Rackham: Obsession, Death and a British Film Star - a new thriller of passion, jealousy and suspense from F.R. Jameson.

The third novel in the Screen Siren Noir series.

ABOUT THE AUTHOR

F.R. Jameson was born in Wales, but now lives with his wife and daughter in London. He writes thrillers; sometimes of the supernatural variety, and sometimes historical, set around the British film industry.

His debut novel, The Wannabes, which contains both horror and British actresses is available for free now from his blog, which you can find at - https://frjameson.com/

On that blog he puts book reviews, film reviews and the occasional writing diary, and you can also find him on Facebook, and follow him on Twitter, Instagram and Pinterest: @frjameson.

Printed in Great Britain
by Amazon